THANKS TO JENNINGS

Anthony Buckeridge started writing radio plays while he was teaching in a prep school after the war. He eventually gave up teaching to write full time. He also acts, chiefly for radio, and has played small parts at Glyndebourne Opera during the season.

The Jennings stories originally began as radio plays on *Children's Hour* in 1948. There are now twenty-four Jennings books. They have been translated into twelve languages, and have sold more than five million copies around the world. They have been read on audio cassette by Stephen Fry, and there have also been two television productions.

These hilarious stories have become classics of children's school fiction, attracting loyal fans of all ages. One of these is the acclaimed playwright Alan Ayckbourn, who has said, "When I was nine or ten I used to roll around on the floor laughing at the Jennings stories. By the time I was eleven I wanted to be Darbishire more than anything in the world."

To Supercool Stevie

unch 'brill' Eoin

*Titles in the Jennings series, available from
Macmillan Children's Books*

Jennings Goes to School
Thanks to Jennings
Especially Jennings
Jennings in Particular
Speaking of Jennings
Trust Jennings
Typically Jennings
The Jennings Report
Jennings of Course
According to Jennings
Jennings at Large
Our Friend Jennings
Jennings and Darbishire
Jennings Unlimited
Take Jennings for Instance
Jennings' Diary
Jennings Again!
That's Jennings!

ANTHONY BUCKERIDGE

Thanks to Jennings

MACMILLAN
CHILDREN'S BOOKS

First published 1957 by William Collins & Sons Co Ltd

This edition published 1996 by Macmillan Children's Books
a division of Macmillan Publishers Limited
25 Eccleston Place London SW1W 9NF
and Basingstoke

Associated companies throughout the world

ISBN 0 333 65524 9

1 3 5 7 9 8 6 4 2

A CIP catalogue record for this book is available from
the British Library

Printed by Mackays of Chatham PLC, Chatham, Kent

Contents

Chapter		page
1	Mr Carter on Duty	1
2	The Furtive Feasters	11
3	Food for Thought	22
4	Small Game Hunt	31
5	The Organised Outing	43
6	Darbishire to the Rescue	55
7	Emergency Call	65
8	Jack Carr's Car Jack	75
9	Assorted Pets	87
10	The Last of F. J. Saunders	101
11	Contributions in Kind	114
12	Catering Arrangements	126
13	No Smoke Without Fire	137
14	An Inspector Calls	149
15	Confusion Below Stairs	160
16	Thanks to Jennings	172

AUTHOR'S NOTE

Each of the Jennings books is a story complete in itself. Apart from the first title, *Jennings Goes to School*, the books can be read in any order.

Anthony Buckeridge

Chapter 1

Mr Carter on Duty

It had always seemed odd to Mr Carter that growing boys could be blissfully happy and thoroughly uncomfortable, both at the same time.

This curious state of affairs could be proved, he maintained, by observing the behaviour of the seventy-nine boarders of Linbury Court School during most of their waking moments. Indeed, the more he observed them the more certain he became that the boys in his charge were numb to all feelings of physical discomfort.

They would scamper barefooted along the ice-cold dormitory flooring, rather than wear the fleecy-lined slippers provided by their parents; they would report to the music room for violin lessons, their fingers glued together with balsawood cement; they would read under the bedclothes by torchlight in conditions of stifling suffocation, and wear their shirts rucked up about their waists in knobbly balls of compressed material . . .

But it was when they were ordered to relax and make themselves comfortable that they *really* excelled in devising methods of self-torture.

For half an hour after lunch each day during the Easter term, the school settled down for a period of compulsory rest. The youngest boys were sent upstairs to lie on their beds; the middle-aged and the seniors, ranging from sprightly ten-year-olds to an elderly thirteen *plus*, retired to common rooms or library where they were expected to digest their lunches and improve their minds by sitting still and reading good books.

In theory, the rest period was a time of quiet repose and meditation. In practice, it was found advisable for the duty master to walk round the buildings to make sure that the silence rule was being observed.

Mr Carter was the master on duty one sunless Monday afternoon in late February. He was a pleasant, quietly-spoken man approaching middle age, with an unhurried manner and a shrewd knowledge of the workings of the youthful mind. He was seldom taken unawares by anything which the boys chose to do; and therefore he showed no surprise as, approaching Dormitory One on his tour of duty, a sound like the twanging of untuned harp strings came wafting out on to the landing.

Mr Carter opened the dormitory door and looked inside. Binns and Blotwell, the youngest boys in the school, were observing the rest period by bouncing up and down on their beds like acrobats on a trampoline. Heedless of warning hisses from the surrounding beds they continued to bounce and flounder, while the vibrating bedsprings groaned in protest . . . *boyng . . . boyng . . . boyng*.

Then Blotwell looked up and saw Mr Carter watching him. With a clumsy back-pedalling movement, the gymnast abandoned his contortions in mid-bound and made a three-point landing on the foot of the bed. A split second later, the airborne Binns thudded down upon his quivering bedstead, his eyelids hurriedly closing in feigned slumber.

"Has it ever occurred to you, Binns and Blotwell, that the whole point of sending you to lie down on your beds is so that you can digest your lunch properly?" Mr Carter inquired.

"Yes, sir," said Blotwell.

"And do you imagine that hurling yourselves into space like a couple of human cannonballs is the best way of aiding digestion?"

Binns opened his eyes. "That's just what we were trying to do really, sir. That suet pudding we had was a bit stodgy, so we were just trying to shake it down a spot further, sir."

"Indeed!" said Mr Carter gravely. And such was his reputation that for the remainder of the rest period Binns and Blotwell lay flat on their beds without stirring. For they liked Mr Carter: they knew they could turn to him in times of trouble. But they also knew that he was not the sort of man to warn anybody twice for the same offence.

Mr Carter continued his tour of the building. In the library on the first floor, he came upon a group of third-form boys festooned about the room in the uncomfortable postures which seemed so much to their liking.

Venables, a tall, thin boy of twelve, was stretched full length on the polished floorboards, squinting through a toy telescope at his library book which he had propped up on the mantelpiece some ten feet away. It was not the easiest way of reading, for the telescope wobbled so unsteadily in his grasp that he had difficulty in keeping the volume in view. To make matters worse, he had to leap to his feet and trot across to the mantelpiece every time he wanted to turn over a page.

Over by the window, C. E. J. Darbishire stood storklike upon one foot, his other leg bent at the knee and supported at the ankle by his right hand. He had put his library book aside and was peering through dusty spectacles at a sodden paper towel which dripped damply upon the windowsill.

Mr Carter's glance travelled round the room and lighted upon an eager, friendly-looking boy of eleven with wide-awake eyes and a fringe of untidy brown hair. At the moment, however, his features were not visible, for he sat crouched on the extreme edge of his chair, leaning forward with shoulders hunched and his head sunk between his knees in a way that imposed the maximum strain upon the seams of his blazer. At first Mr Carter thought that the boy must be feeling faint. Then he noticed the open book on the floor and realised that the reader was bending forward in this curious doubled-up position in order to focus his gaze upon the printed page.

Apart from hanging upside down like a two-toed sloth, Mr Carter could think of no more uncomfortable method of reading a book.

"Jennings!" he called.

The reader uncoiled himself and jumped to his feet. "Sir?"

"You'll get a rush of blood to your head if you sit like that. Wouldn't it be possible to hold the book in your hands instead of laying it on the floor between your feet?"

"Yes, I suppose it would really, sir. I never thought of that," Jennings answered. In a burst of enthusiasm he went on. "It's a really great book, too, sir. It's got an article on how to run your own menagerie. You know, sir – white mice, tame rats, guinea-pigs, tropical fish and things; and even carrier pigeons, sir."

"Really," said Mr Carter. It did not require much mental effort on his part to guess where the conversation was leading.

"Yes, sir, and I was just thinking if the Head would give us per, sir, we could . . ."

"Give you *what*, Jennings?"

"Permission, sir. If he'd let us make some cages and get

some pets, like, say, for instance, a few white rabbits, sir, we could . . ."

The enthusiasm ebbed from his voice and tailed off into silence at the expression on Mr Carter's face.

"It's no good, Jennings," the master said. "Not in term time, anyway. You can keep all the pets you want in the holidays, but the headmaster certainly wouldn't allow you to turn the school into a private zoo, especially after what happened last time. I should have thought you would have known that, considering you were largely to blame for his decision."

Why were masters so keen on raking up old history, Jennings wondered? Why must they keep recalling awkward moments of the past that were best forgotten? It was true that the ban had been imposed after his ill-fated attempt to give a pet goldfish some health-giving exercise in the school swimming bath. But, after all, that had happened years and years ago – well, a couple of terms, anyway. Now that time had healed the wound, perhaps the headmaster could be persuaded to change his mind.

"We'd look after them ever so carefully, sir," Jennings pleaded. "We wouldn't let them out in the dormitory, or anywhere like that, sir."

"I should think not indeed," said Mr Carter, with a mental shudder at the prospect of classrooms and lobbies cluttered ankle deep with small furry animals scurrying to freedom. "In any case, Jennings, it's quite out of the question. After the first week or so, when the novelty had worn off, you'd find your pets were more bother than they were worth. Think of all the trouble you'd have finding enough for them to eat."

"Oh, that wouldn't be too difficult, sir," Jennings persisted. He knew that there was small chance of the ban

5

being lifted. Yet his mind refused to leave the topic alone, for he enjoyed making plans, even though they might never be carried out. "We could feed them on crusts of bread and things, and give them plenty of healthy greenstuff, such as . . . such as . . . well, like, say, for instance . . ."

"Mustard and cress," Darbishire chimed in triumphantly from across the room. He picked up the sheet of wet paper towel, trotted over to Mr Carter and held out the sodden object for his inspection.

"That's what I'm growing on this paper, sir," he explained, as the master recoiled from the mossy green substance thrust under his nose. "It's easy, really. You only have to sprinkle some seed on to the paper and keep it wet, and it comes up like a house on fire, sir. Actually I was growing it to make salads with, but I wouldn't mind doing an extra supply for a private menagerie."

"I've just been telling Jennings to abandon the idea," Mr Carter pointed out.

"Yes, I know, sir. I heard you." Like his friend, Darbishire saw no reason to draw the line too clearly between make-believe and reality. For this was one of those practical daydreams, capable of achievement if only grown-ups would look at it from a sensible angle. "I know we can't *really* do it, sir: I was just thinking what fun it would be if we *could*." Chattily, he prattled on, "It's ever so easy to grow mustard and cress on towels, sir. And you can grow it on wet flannel, too, if you like."

Jennings snorted at this display of ignorance. "You can't, you know."

"Why not?"

"Because Matron won't let you, that's why. I grew quite a good crop on my face flannel a few weeks ago, and she made me wash it all off just as it was ready for harvesting."

"Too bad," Mr Carter sympathised. "All the same, I can see Matron's point of view. We should have the bathroom looking like an allotment if everybody's sponge bag started to sprout vegetables."

As he left the library a few minutes later, the master noticed that Jennings was once again crouching over the book at his feet, absorbed in the details of running a private menagerie.

Mr Carter was not worried. Quite apart from the headmaster's ban, he felt certain that the boys would have little chance during term time of acquiring any form of animal life larger than a stray earwig . . . But for once Mr Carter was wrong.

Jennings looked up from his book as the duty master left the room. "It tells you here how to make a rabbit hutch out of a tea chest," he observed.

"What's the good of that if you haven't got a rabbit?" Darbishire grumbled. "It's a mouldy chizz. You're never allowed to do anything sensible at school."

His mouth drooped in a grimace of disapproval. Vague and impractical by nature, Darbishire was content as a rule to leave plans of action to his more forceful colleague.

"It'd be a good idea to make the hutch though – just in case," Jennings said.

"In case of what?"

"Well, suppose we found a stray one," Jennings argued. "We could keep it somewhere like, say, for instance, behind the shoelockers, and nobody would ever know it was there."

Darbishire shook his head. "I can just see *that* happening!"

"I only said *suppose*," Jennings pointed out. In the realm of make-believe the most fantastic things could be imagined without landing anybody in trouble. "I didn't say we could actually get one. I was just thinking what a lobsterous scheme it would be to keep a secret menagerie that nobody knew about."

"So long as you're only *supposing*, you can plan to keep a flock of elephants in the bike shed, if you want to," Darbishire conceded. "But if you honestly think you'll ever really find a spare pet wandering round the building in search of an owner you must be crazy. It's one of those things that just couldn't happen."

Darbishire spoke with conviction. But then, he had no means of foreseeing the future any more than Mr Carter!

The bell for the end of the rest period was sounding as the duty master made his way along to the headmaster's study at the far end of the building, and knocked on the door.

Unlike his pupils, Mr Pemberton-Oakes, the headmaster, preferred to spend the half hour after lunch in a state of restful coma, from which he awoke refreshed to face the rigours of the afternoon.

"Ah, come in, Carter, come in," said Mr Pemberton-Oakes, struggling back into full wakefulness with an effort of will. "I'm glad you looked in. As a matter of fact I was just on the point of – of . . ."

The headmaster searched his mind. What on earth *had* he been meaning to do just before he dropped off into his after-lunch doze? Something important, no doubt: but for the life of him he couldn't remember what it was. Vaguely he finished up, "I was just – ah – pondering over various matters of school routine."

"That's what I came to see you about," Mr Carter replied. "I'd rather like to organise an expedition for the Camera Club some time during the next few weeks. So far this term the weather's been so bad that they've had practically no chance to take photographs."

A photographic expedition? The headmaster pursed his lips and raised one eyebrow as he considered the suggestion. "Why not! Perhaps you and Wilkins would take a party into Dunhambury some half-holiday when we have no football fixture."

"Yes, of course."

"Splendid! I'm sure the boys will find a wealth of suitable subjects in an historic town like Dunhambury. There are the sixteenth-century castle walls, for instance; the seventeenth-century market cross; the eighteenth-century town hall, the – er . . ." A sweep of the hand included all the rest of the architectural features, from the nineteenth-century fire station to the twentieth-century petrol pumps.

Mr Carter consulted his pocket diary and noted there was no football match arranged for the second Wednesday in March. "Camera Club. Visit to Dunhambury," he wrote.

He was about to take his leave when the headmaster called him back. Mr Pemberton-Oakes's brain, refreshed by sleep, was now working with its usual zest, and he had just remembered the matter which had eluded him a few minutes earlier.

"By the way, Carter. I've arranged for my accountant and one of his clerks to come down tomorrow to start the annual audit of the school accounts," he said. "It may take them several days, and I can't let them use my study as I shall be needing it, so I was wondering whether you'd mind if they worked in the staff common room?"

"I see no objection," Mr Carter agreed. "Where will they have their lunch? In the dining-hall with the rest of the school?"

Mr Pemberton-Oakes pondered the query. "Perhaps the simplest plan would be for Matron to take it along to the common room for them. Then they can have it when they're ready, and they won't have to bother about observing school mealtimes."

"Very well then, I'll arrange that with Matron. It certainly seems the simplest way of doing it."

In point of fact, all the arrangements which Mr Carter had made in the half hour after lunch seemed simple enough. He had given a timely reminder about the keeping of pets; he had agreed to organise an outing of the Camera Club; and he could see no reason why the chartered accountants should not eat their lunch in the staff-room.

It was not often that Mr Carter made an unwise decision. But on this occasion he made three errors of judgement in the space of thirty minutes.

Chapter 2

The Furtive Feasters

The first hint of trouble occurred during lunch the following day, while Jennings was helping himself to salt. The top of the upturned salt cellar dropped off and landed on his plate. Meat, cabbage and potatoes were smothered in the sudden avalanche, while granules of salt absorbed the last remnant of the gravy.

By the time he had struggled through his first course and was halfway through the prunes and custard which followed, Jennings was overcome by a raging thirst.

"Water, please . . . Water, please!" he called loudly down the table.

There was no response. Venables, seated within arm's distance of the jug, was too busy chasing a slippery prune round the edge of his plate to take any notice; and Temple, seated beside him, was vainly trying to straighten a fork suffering from ingrowing prongs.

"Water, please . . . Water, please!" came the urgent summons. "Hey, Temple, Venables, wake up and sling the jug down this end of the table. I've asked you forty-nine million times already."

Venables speared the slippery prune and bolted it quickly in the hope of achieving a second helping. "Quite good, these prunes, aren't they, Temple?" he observed.

"Not too gruesome," his friend agreed, counting the stones to make sure he had received his just portion. "Tinker, tailor, soldier, sailor . . ."

"Oh, this is hopeless!" Jennings protested. "I shall die of thirst in a minute. I've asked you fifty million times already. For the fifty million and first time, water, please . . . Water, please! . . . *Water, please!*"

His voice rose to a shout, cutting across the babble of conversation around him. At once everyone stopped talking, startled into silence by the sudden uproar. At the top table the headmaster stretched out his hand and tinkled the little bell he used when he wished to attract the boys' attention.

Seventy-nine heads swivelled round to face the headmaster's table.

"Which boy was responsible for that noise?" he demanded.

Jennings stood up. "It was me, sir, please, sir."

The headmaster winced. "You mean 'It was *I*,' Jennings."

Jennings hesitated, wondering whether the headmaster was unjustly accusing himself of creating the disturbance, but a moment's reflection convinced him that Mr Pemberton-Oakes was merely quibbling over a point of grammar.

"Yes, sir. I mean it was I, sir. I wanted another glass of water and no one would pass me the jug."

"That is no excuse for unruly and ungentlemanly behaviour at the luncheon table. If there's any further breach of manners, Form Three will finish the meal in silence." The headmaster tinkled the little bell as a sign that the incident was now closed, and a restrained buzz of conversation broke out once more all over the room.

"You are a crazy clodpoll, Jennings, nearly getting us all put on silence," Temple complained. He would have said more, but at that moment Matron rose from her chair and made her way towards the serving hatch.

"Ooh, Matron, are there any seconds, please?" Temple asked eagerly as she approached.

"I don't know yet," she told him. "I shall have to see whether the staff would like some more first."

Temple turned to his neighbour with a shrug. "That means there won't be any left for us."

"Mouldy chizz," Venables agreed.

"It's always the same. It's always the staff who get the second helpings," lamented Atkinson from across the table. He wagged an ink-stained forefinger at his grumbling colleagues. "It'll be different one day, though. Just you wait, that's all."

Along both sides of the table, the boys watched with growing concern as one master after another smilingly accepted a second portion of prunes and custard.

"Tut! Look at Old Wilkie shovelling them down!" Temple said with feeling. "Anyone would think he'd had nothing to eat since the Wars of the Roses. I bet you a million pounds there won't be any left when it comes to our turn."

His forecast was not entirely correct. Nobody was actually refused a second helping, though by the time the Third Form table was served the size of the portions was diminishing in an alarming fashion. Jennings, who was the last to be served, was given the smallest helping of all.

"Two prunes! Two measly prunes!" he complained when the plate was set before him. "How do they expect us to work in class till our brains sizzle when we're starving with hunger and parching with thirst all the time!"

Darbishire, seated beside his friend, bent forward to examine the despised portion. "And they're not even proper-sized ones," he sympathised. "Look at that tiddly little shrivelled-up specimen. You'd need a microscope to get that one in focus. It's so small you can only see it in a strong light."

"Like to borrow my pocket telescope, Jennings?" Venables inquired facetiously.

Rather to his surprise the offer was accepted.

"Yes, I certainly would! I don't see why I should ruin my eyesight looking for a prune that's barely visible to the naked eye."

Venables took the telescope from his pocket and willing hands passed it down the table.

A ripple of amusement followed as Jennings put the instrument to his eye and focused it upon his plate. Conscious of the stir he was creating amongst his colleagues, he began playing up to their interest with exaggerated gestures and facial contortions.

"I'm a big prune-hunter, searching the African jungle for a rare specimen known as the lesser shrivelled prune!" he announced in tones of mock gravity as he polished the lens of the telescope on his tie. The ripple of amusement grew louder as his audience settled down to watch the panto-mime devised for their amusement. This was a comedy after their own hearts.

"I will now proceed to give my famous demonstration of prune-stalking. I focus ye telescope on ye plate, like so . . . Yes, I think I can see it wallowing in the shallows of the custard swamp - the smallest specimen of prune known to science."

"Mind it doesn't escape," Darbishire cautioned, as the ripple swelled to a wave of laughter.

"Ssh! Quiet, Darbi! You'll frighten it away!" Jennings whispered with a ludicrous gesture of caution. "Stand back, everybody! I am now going into the attack armed only with a bent-pronged school fork."

The bell at the top table rang out more loudly than before.

"Jennings!"

There was no doubt from the tone of his voice that Mr Pemberton-Oakes was extremely annoyed.

"What are you doing with a telescope at the luncheon table?"

Jennings' chair scraped on the floor as he rose to his feet. Carried away by the success of his entertainment, he had not realised that his antics had been observed from the far end of the room. He stood there silent and humbled, feeling rather foolish.

"I asked you, Jennings, what you were doing with that telescope!"

"I was – er – I was just looking at my prune through it, sir."

It was not a very convincing answer and it failed to satisfy the headmaster.

"And may one inquire the reason for this extraordinary behaviour?"

What could he say? It was impossible to explain out loud to a hushed room a joke that was no longer funny, especially when faced with the headmaster's stare of disapproval.

"I don't know, sir," he mumbled.

"If that ill-mannered exhibition was your idea of being funny, Jennings, it was a jest in extremely bad taste," said Mr Pemberton-Oakes. "You will eat your meals in silence for a week. Boys who behave in that way don't deserve the same privileges as civilised human beings . . . Leave the room at once!"

"Bad luck, Jen," whispered Darbishire as his friend, low in spirit, turned to leave the dining-hall.

It was not that he minded being sent out, Jennings told himself as he stood outside in the corridor, for the meal was nearly over and his period of exile would not last long. But the prospect of eating in silence for a whole week seemed a big price to pay for a joke that hadn't quite come off.

He had not been waiting long when the door behind him opened, and Matron emerged from the dining-hall carrying a tray stacked with plates and steaming dishes for the accountants' lunches in the staff-room. She had been in the kitchen organising the extra meals while Jennings was being taken to task by the headmaster, and so she knew nothing of the punishment that had been imposed.

"What are you doing out here, Jennings?" she asked. "You haven't been sent out, have you?"

He nodded.

"Why? What were you doing?"

It was easier to reply to the question this time, for Matron was a likeable sort of person, young enough to lend a sympathetic ear to his troubles.

"I was looking at my pudding through a telescope, Matron. I was pretending I couldn't see it without." Anxious to change the subject to a less embarrassing topic, he hurried on. "That tray looks terribly heavy, Matron. Would you like me to carry it up to the sick-room for you?"

"No, thank you. I can manage," she replied, as she moved away down the corridor. "In any case, it's not going to the sick-room. These are just some extra lunches I'm taking along to the staff common room."

Extra lunches? . . . Extra lunches for the *staff common room*?

Jennings gaped after her in amazement as the significance sank into his mind. Knowing nothing of the hungry accountants awaiting their midday repast, he could think of only one explanation to fit the facts. It was a disturbing thought. Very disturbing indeed!

A thunderous rumbling from behind the dining-hall door announced that seventy-eight boys were pushing back their chairs and rising to their feet. A few moments later, Darbishire, Venables and Atkinson appeared at the head of the throng which came surging out into the corridor.

"Oh, there you are, Jen. Bad luck getting sent out like that," Darbishire began chattily. He fumbled in his pocket and produced an off-white handkerchief screwed up into a ball. "Here you are, look. I've got those two prunes you didn't finish, if you still want them?"

Jennings appeared to be in the grip of some powerful emotion.

"Thanks, Darbi, but I couldn't eat them now," he said in a strained voice. "They'd turn to ashes in my mouth."

"They're practically ashes already – especially the little shrivelled one," Darbishire observed, as he unwrapped the off-white handkerchief. "If you ask me, school cooking is the last . . ."

He broke off at the sight of his friend's expression. "What's up, Jen?"

"Listen, Darbi. And you lot. I've just made an important discovery." Jennings' tone was grave and he spoke in the hushed whisper of a conspirator with a secret to reveal. "There's something going on in this school that you don't know about."

His audience pressed closer, agog for information.

"It's pretty serious, too . . . *The masters are secret eaters!*"

It took a few moments for the news to sink in.

"Secret eaters! What on earth are you waffling about?" Venables demanded.

"Well, Mr Carter and Mr Wilkins and the Head and all of them have just had lunch with us, haven't they?"

"I should say so. They had first go at the second helpings, too," Temple complained as he came up and joined the group.

"Ah, yes, but do you know what they're going to do now? They're going to go and have another full meal in the staff-room right away!"

The announcement caused an immediate sensation.

"Hey, that's not fair!"

It seemed that there were no depths to which adult injustice would not sink.

"Are you quite sure, Jen?" Darbishire asked in tones of horrified disbelief.

"Of course I'm sure. I can prove it. Matron's just gone staggering along there with a massive great tray piled to the ceiling with boiled beef and prunes and custard and things. And what's more, she actually admitted where she was taking it."

"Phew! Furtive feasting!" exclaimed Temple. "So that's why they always rush off to the staff-room after lunch, is it!"

"Of course it is! I've unmasked the whole plot."

By now Jennings was aflame with righteous indignation. "Just think of it! All through lunch the masters sit there smiling to themselves because they know there's another whacking great meal waiting for them, while we have to make do on undersized prunes and glasses of water . . . And we don't even get *that* when some people are just too lazy to pass the jug!"

Temple ignored the reference to his table manners,

"Ghastly! It makes me feel empty inside, just to think about it," he said, tightening his belt to show the extent of his suffering.

"And for all we know they do it after the other meals as well," Darbishire said as fresh possibilities occurred to him. "I wouldn't be surprised if they had two breakfasts, two lunches, two teas, and two suppers. Eight meals a day! . . . Fifty-four meals a week! Wow!"

"Seven eights are fifty-six," corrected Venables, whose mathematics was of a slightly higher standard.

"That's even worse then," exclaimed Darbishire. "What couldn't I do with fifty-six meals a week!"

Venables, alone, was disinclined to believe the theory that the staff were engaged in a conspiracy.

"We've only got Jennings' word for it," he maintained. "The only way we could prove it would be to march *slap-bang* into the staff-room after a meal and catch them red-handed."

Darbishire shook his head. "We couldn't do that. We'd have to knock first and wait for an answer."

In his mind's eye he tried to picture the scene of chaos and confusion in the staff-room that would follow an unexpected rapping on the door. Plates would be hurriedly concealed behind the bookcase, cutlery dropped into the wastepaper basket and the window flung open to dispel the appetising aroma. Then, and only then, would the door be opened a few cautious inches by some master swallowing the last remnant of food and furtively wiping his fingers on his handkerchief.

It was certainly difficult – almost impossible – to believe . . . But how exciting it would be if it were true!

Jennings was too intrigued by his own brilliant reasoning to worry about the weak points in his theory.

"It all fits in, doesn't it?" he said. "No wonder the masters are always telling us to hurry up with our lunch. I'd do the same if I'd got a secret meal waiting for me."

"So would I," Darbishire agreed. "Of course I can understand Old Wilkie being a furtive feaster, but I can't get over Mr Carter. It just shows you never know with grown-ups."

By this time the last stragglers were leaving the dining-hall. At the tail end of the procession came Mr Carter and Mr Wilkins who had remained behind to confer about the arrangements for the afternoon.

L. P. Wilkins, MA (Cantab), known out of earshot as Old Wilkie, was a large, burly man, with a loud voice and a heavy footstep. An impatient manner concealed the fact that he was, in reality, fond of the boys whom he taught; but unlike his colleague, Mr Carter, he judged youthful conduct from a grown-up point of view, and could seldom understand why boys should choose to behave in a way which appeared to him to be utterly lacking in reason.

"Come along now, you boys. Don't block up the corridor," he boomed in his deep, loud-hailer of a voice. "It's time you were all upstairs in the library for rest period."

Jennings favoured Mr Wilkins with what he hoped was the inscrutable smile of one who knows all. The performance was not a success.

"What on earth's the matter with you, Jennings? Are you feeling ill?" the master demanded.

"No, sir."

"Then stop gawping like a half-witted village idiot." He turned to the rest of the group. "I can't think why you boys *will* hang about outside the dining-hall after lunch is over. Anyone would think you were hoping for another meal."

Jennings and Darbishire exchanged glances. Here, surely, was further proof that furtive feasting was the subject uppermost in Mr Wilkins' mind.

Jennings made no comment as he led the way upstairs to the library. But Darbishire, following at his heels, could read his friend's mind as clearly as though he were a character in a cartoon advertisement with a balloon of thought floating in space above his head.

"Aha!" read the thought-balloon in bold, black type. "Little does Sir know that his crafty secret has been discovered."

Chapter 3

Food for Thought

The rest period in the library that afternoon was remarkable for its air of restlessness. As the news of Jennings' discovery spread round the room, his theory gained many supporters. Even those who doubted it tried their hardest to believe, for the faint suspicion that the rumour might contain some grain of truth gave them a feeling of grievance that was, somehow, very satisfying.

"Still, you can't prove it," argued Bromwich, a dark, curly-haired third-former who, with Venables, headed a noisy minority of disbelievers. "Old Jennings is always getting things mixed up. I bet this is just another of his bat-witted ideas."

"No, it isn't. I bet you what you like I'm right, and what's more, I'll prove it."

"How?"

"Well, I'll – er – I'll . . ." Jennings searched his mind for some way of convincing the sceptics. Vaguely he finished up, "I'll set a trap for them. You see if I don't!"

"And then what?" Bromwich jeered. "Even supposing you're right, you can't do anything about it. They can eat till they're blue in the face for all you . . ."

"Oh, don't be so wet, Bromo, you gruesome specimen!" Jennings broke in. "You're only jealous because you didn't think of it first."

"No, I'm not. And anyway, if I'm a gruesome specimen

you're the same, only wetter, so bad luck."

"No, I'm not; so double bad luck to you, and no returns."

The debate continued for some minutes at this high level of oratory and brilliant repartee until Atkinson, arriving late for the rest period, burst into the library with a warning of impending danger.

"Ssh! Look out! Old Wilkie'll be round in a minute. I saw him beetling out of the staff-room with Mr Carter. Heading this way, by the looks of it."

The debaters ceased wrangling. Books were hurriedly opened and frowns of concentration furrowed the brows of the studious readers.

"They've wolfed their secret meal down pretty quickly, haven't they?" Darbishire observed, flicking over the pages of his library book.

"Well, of course. Look at all the practice they get," Temple pointed out. "Besides, they daren't be too long over it in case we smell a rat."

When Mr Wilkins and Mr Carter entered the room a few moments later they found the occupants engaged in silent reading, crouching and perching over their books in the uncomfortable attitudes of their choice.

Under cover of his library book, Bromwich caught Jennings' eye and mouthed quietly, "Now's your chance. Prove it, if you're so clever."

Jennings pursed his lips in thought. He had a bag of liquorice allsorts in his pocket. He would see how the furtive feasters reacted to the sight of yet more food.

"Would you like a sweet, sir?" he inquired politely, proffering the screwed-up bag to Mr Carter.

"That's very kind of you, Jennings, but I don't think I could manage one at the moment. Too soon after lunch."

Darbishire shot a keen glance at Mr Carter. Exactly *which* lunch was the master referring to, he wondered? Then he watched as Jennings held out the bag to Mr Wilkins who seemed rather surprised at the unexpected display of generosity.

"Thank you, Jennings. I think I could find a small corner for a liquorice allsort. Thank you very much." With some difficulty Mr Wilkins loosened one of the sticky objects from the congealed mass at the bottom of the bag.

"H'm. Extremely good, these sweets, Carter," he said as he put one in his mouth. "You should have tried them."

Mr Carter laughed. "I couldn't eat another thing," he protested.

As the masters left the room Jennings turned to Bromwich with a cry of triumph. "There you are! What did I tell you! You heard what they said. Isn't that proof enough?"

Bromwich looked blank. "It doesn't prove anything at all. One of them accepted and the other one didn't, so you're back where you started."

"Don't be so thick, Bromo! Mr Carter said 'No' because he's so full already that he hasn't even got room for a liquorice allsort," Jennings explained. "Therefore he must have had two lunches."

"But Old Wilkie did take one!"

"That just shows how greedy he is. Two lunches and he *still* isn't satisfied!"

Temple nodded his assent. "It stands to reason whichever way you look at it. Jennings' theory is bound to be right."

There were some who doubted the logic of the argument. And gradually their resentment cooled and they lost interest as their thoughts turned to more immediate matters. By bedtime most of the boys had dismissed the topic from their minds.

Not so, Jennings! He talked a great deal about his discovery as he sat up in bed in Dormitory Four that evening, waiting for the master on duty to come round and put the lights out. What impressed him most was the brilliance of his deduction, which he seemed to think more important than the truth of what he had deduced.

"It came to me in a flash, Darbi, as soon as Matron told me where she was taking the tray. 'Aha,' I thought . . ."

"All right, all right," protested Darbishire, foaming at the mouth with pink toothpaste. "That's the fifty millionth time you've told me you thought 'Aha'. What are you going to do about it? March up to Old Wilkie and tell him he ought to go on a diet?"

"Of course not. I was only thinking that if the masters can do that and get away with it, why shouldn't we do the same?"

"You must be crazy!" chimed in Atkinson from the farther washbasin. "Where are we going to get fifty-six meals a week from, for a kick-off?"

"We could have just *one*, couldn't we?" Jennings argued. "A really first-class, secret feast with so much to eat that we shouldn't feel hungry till – well, till the next meal, anyway."

The idea had possibilities. "Where should we have it?" queried Venables, showing approval for the first time.

"Here in the dorm, of course. Just us five."

"Yes, why not?" Temple demanded. "We could have it after lights out, while Old Wilkie and Co are tucking into their second secret supper."

By now the plan had gained the support of all five members of Dormitory Four.

"I've got a tin of sardines we could have to start off with," Temple suggested.

"And I've got some mustard and cress I'm growing on wet kitchen paper," added Darbishire.

Jennings dismissed the offers with a snort of contempt.

"Sardines! Mustard and kitchen paper!" he said scornfully. "That sort of stuff is all right for a snack, but if we're going to lay on a really first-class banquet, surely we can find something better than mouldy sardines and paper-towel sandwiches."

"Hear, hear! Let's have a proper cooked meal," Venables suggested, without a thought for the difficulties involved. "Meat and potatoes, suet dumplings, blancmange; the lot – all hot!"

Darbishire shook his head sadly. "It's all very well to talk. Where on earth could we cook a meal like that?"

It was Jennings, as usual, who supplied the answer. "Down in the boiler room, of course. We could mix it all up together in a sort of stew and pop it on the furnace at the beginning of prep. Then, when the masters have all gone in to supper, one of us could nip down from the dorm and retrieve it."

"Good!" cried Atkinson, swinging his sponge bag round his head. "That's settled then. All we've got to do is to . . ."

"Yes, but half a minute: where are we going to get the meat and stuff from? Those sort of things don't grow on trees, you know."

Temple had certainly raised a point of some importance. Bank balances were low at that period of the term, and a feast on this grand scale would entail a considerable outlay.

This time it was Atkinson who came to the rescue. "You can leave all that side of it to me," he offered in a burst of generosity. "My grandmother's coming down to see me on Thursday week, and she always brings masses of food."

"Raw meat and potatoes?" queried Darbishire, doubtfully.

"Well, no, not as a rule," Atkinson confessed. "But you can buy tins of Irish stew already mixed; and if I wrote and asked her to bring a couple I bet she wouldn't ask what I wanted them for. Then all we'd have to do would be to stand the tins on the boiler and take them off when they were ready."

Atkinson's suggestion made everything a great deal easier. No need to worry about saucepans and cooking fat! A tin opener would provide all that was required in the way of utensils.

The offer was accepted with thanks and the banquet arranged for the following Friday week. It was unlikely that any of them would forget such an important function, but to be on the safe side Jennings entered the engagement in his diary, with a note of the menu to be enjoyed. For security reasons he spelled the words backwards. There was always a chance that the diary might fall into the wrong hands. *Unem*, he wrote, *Owt snit fo Hsiri wets*.

The first major setback occurred two days later when Atkinson retired to the sick-room suffering from tonsilitis. The news cast a pall of gloom over Dormitory Four.

"Mouldy swizz. Just like Atkinson to go and bish up the issue," Temple fumed. "I've a good mind to bash him up the next time I see him."

"A fat lot of good that'd do. He'd call the whole thing off, if you did," Jennings pointed out. "We'll just have to postpone the feast, that's all. We'll have it as soon as he comes back into school again."

"But what about the secret food supplies?" Darbishire

queried. "We don't even know whether he's written for them or not."

As it happened, Atkinson wrote to his grandmother on his second day in the sick-room, when he was feeling a little better. He told her that he had been placed on a light diet and had difficulty in swallowing, and would she kindly bring several large tins of Irish stew when she came to see him.

Mrs Atkinson, senior, decided that the boy must be delirious. Nothing else could account for such an extraordinary request. Accordingly, she ignored his plea and set out by car for Linbury on the following Thursday week with a basket of grapes and a bottle of barley water.

When she arrived at the market town of Dunhambury, some five miles from the school, it occurred to her that the invalid might like something to cheer him up during his period of convalescence. What should she buy? . . . A jigsaw puzzle? . . . A card game of some sort?

She stopped the car and looked out of the window along the crowded High Street in search of a toy shop. She was disappointed. A butcher's shop, a café and an ironmonger's first met her eye; and she was about to drive on when she noticed a small shop with packets of bird seed in the window and dog leads festooned round the door. Above the shop front was inscribed: *Dunhambury Pet Stores. H. Fagg, Propr.*

It looked promising. Mrs Atkinson, senior, alighted from the car and made her way across the road in search of a suitable present for her convalescent grandson.

Mr Wilkins was pinning a notice on the noticeboard when Atkinson's grandmother came down the stairs from the sick-room and crossed the hall to the front door.

"Good afternoon, Mr Wilkins. I've just been up to see Robin," she greeted him. "He certainly seems quite cheerful."

"Splendid," said Mr Wilkins, racking his brains for a clue to the visitor's identity. There were at least six Robins in the school and this middle-aged woman might have been the grandmother of any of them. Parslow and Thompson were both in the sick-room, he remembered, the latter recovering from a minor injury received on the football pitch.

Mr Wilkins risked a question. "How's Robin's sprained ankle getting on?" he asked pleasantly.

The visitor looked surprised. "I didn't know he had one. He's supposed to be suffering from tonsilitis."

"Yes, yes of course. Tonsilitis," Mr Wilkins replied, mentally crossing off Thompson from the list of probable Robins. Obviously the lady must be some relative of Parslow's.

"I've brought a few things for him," Mrs Atkinson went on, indicating some parcels on the hall table. "Matron appears to be out this afternoon, so I left them down here for her to take charge of when she comes back. I haven't told Robin what I've brought, as I don't know what he's allowed to have and what he isn't, and I shouldn't like the dear boy to be disappointed."

"That's all right. I'll see he gets them," Mr Wilkins assured her as he escorted her to the main entrance. "Goodbye, Mrs – er – um – Mrs Parslow.

"Mrs Atkinson," she corrected.

"Yes, yes, of course. Stupid of me. I beg your pardon."

Mr Wilkins closed the door and returned to the hall. He would take the parcels along to Matron's room at once, he decided; there would just be time before . . .

Suddenly Mr Wilkins have a little jump and drew back his hand. A high-pitched squeak had come from one of the parcels, a square wooden box with holes punched in the lid.

There was something wrong somewhere! What article of invalid diet could possibly emit a sound like a violin's *E*-string, he wondered. Cautiously he prised back the lid, and then opened his eyes in amazement. From the bottom of the box, a small, white guinea-pig returned his stare unwinkingly.

"I – I – *Corwumph!*" Mr Wilkins slammed down the lid, pounded across the hall and hurled open the front door.

He was just in time to see the last puff of smoke from the exhaust pipe of Mrs Atkinson's car as it rounded the bend of the drive.

Really, some grandmothers were the limit! Mr Wilkins fumed to himself as he gathered up the parcels from the hall table. No idea of school rules! No idea at all! As though he hadn't enough to do without taking care of confiscated livestock . . . Why, if things went on like this he might as well buy himself a shiny peaked cap and apply for a job at the zoo!

Chapter 4

Small Game Hunt

When Mr Carter paid a visit to his colleague's study during break the next morning, he was surprised to find Mr Wilkins crawling round the room on all fours.

"What on earth are you doing, Wilkins? Inspecting the floorboards for dry rot?" he inquired.

The crawler looked up from his labours. "I'm looking for something," he grunted.

"What is it you've lost?"

"Well, as a matter of fact, I've . . ." Mr Wilkins hesitated as though doubtful whether his explanation would be believed. "Well, I know it sounds improbable, Carter, but between you and me I've lost a guinea-pig."

Mr Carter blinked. "I never knew you kept guinea-pigs."

"I *don't* keep guinea-pigs," protested Mr Wilkins, shocked by this monstrous accusation. "I've never kept guinea-pigs in my life. I can't stand the sight of the things."

"Then how did you manage to lose something you never had?"

Mr Wilkins replaced the carpet and rose to his feet. "I just happened to be in charge of one, that's all."

The explanation was simple. The misguided kindness of Atkinson's grandmother had been reported to the headmaster who had lost no time in writing her a letter pointing out the breach of regulations, and asking if she would kindly come back and remove the offending animal from

31

the school premises as soon as possible. Pending her arrival, the letter continued, the guinea-pig would be placed in the safe care of one of the masters.

"And now the wretched rodent has escaped," Mr Wilkins ended up bitterly. "It was sitting in its box pruning its ridiculous whiskers when I went into school this morning, and when I came back just now I found the lid half off and the box empty."

"If the door was shut, it must be still in the room somewhere," Mr Carter said, poking about vaguely behind the bookcase.

"Yes, but I'm not sure the door *was* shut. In fact, now I come to think about it, I believe I left it ajar," Mr Wilkins admitted. "In any case, how was I to know that an undersized shrimp of an animal like that would have enough brute strength to push the lid back."

"It was probably hungry. Did you give it anything to eat?"

Mr Wilkins shrugged. "Nothing very suitable, I'm afraid. The only edible object I could find in my room was a compressed-looking liquorice allsort that some wretched third-former had left between the pages of his history book. But the brute wouldn't look at it. It just wrinkled its nose up and turned away."

Mr Carter abandoned his search behind the bookcase. "It's obviously gone off to look for something a little more to its liking," he decided. "You'd better lay in a good stock of raw cabbage leaves to feed it on when you find it."

"Yes, I will – *if* I find it," Mr Wilkins grumbled. The prospect of organising a small game hunt in the darker corners of the building did little to cheer his spirits. At the door he turned and said, "It really is too bad, Carter. As though I hadn't enough to do, teaching boys, without looking after their grandmothers' livestock as well. It's high time these old ladies learnt to obey school rules."

Mr Carter refused to take the matter seriously. "Good hunting, Wilkins!" he said with a smile. "Don't forget to bait the trap with something really appetising. If I meet you tiptoeing along the corridor trailing a cabbage leaf on a piece of string, I shall know the chase has begun in earnest."

"*Doh!*" An explosive sound like the application of a compressed air brake forced its way through Mr Wilkins' lips. The door slammed behind him and his heavy footsteps echoed along the corridor as he set off on his quest.

If only Mr Wilkins had turned to the left instead of the right on leaving his study, his search might have ended more quickly. For then he would have arrived in the shoeroom in the basement to find Jennings staring with puzzled wonder at a small guinea-pig with pink eyes, scrabbling about behind the shoelockers in the hope of finding something to eat.

But Mr Wilkins took the wrong turning and, as luck would have it, it was Darbishire, hurrying down in search of a missing house-shoe, who came across his friend grinning with surprise and excitement.

"What are you doing skulking down here, Jen?" he began loudly. "We're all supposed to be outside on the . . ."

"Ssh! Quiet, Darbi!" Jennings spun round with a gesture of silence. "And for goodness' sake keep your feet still. You sound as though you're marking time in diver's boots!"

"What on earth are you waffling about? All I said was . . ."

Darbishire stopped abruptly. For at that moment he

caught sight of two pink eyes winking up at him from the entrance of Bromwich's shoelocker.

"Wow!" he shouted in glee. "A real, live guinea-pig! Hey, Jen, where on earth did he spring from?"

"Shut up, Darbi," Jennings ordered in a hoarse whisper. "Don't broadcast it all over the place at the top of your voice. We don't want everyone to know. Think of the hoo-hah there'd be if Old Wilkie, or someone, knew there was a guinea-pig on the premises."

"Yes, but how did it get *on* the premises?" Darbishire persisted in a lower tone. "It isn't yours, is it?"

"Good heavens, no! I just came down here to look for an apple I tucked away in my shoelocker yesterday, and there it was on the floor."

"Your apple?"

"No, you clodpoll, the guinea-pig." Jennings wrinkled his nose in perplexity as he knelt down to inspect the animal at close quarters. "He can't possibly belong to anyone in the school because of the rule about pets. And I can't see any of the masters going in for livestock."

"What about Matron? She's an animal-lover. She's got a cat already, so why . . ."

"All the more reason for it not being hers. A guinea-pig wouldn't go down well with a cat."

"It might go down *too* well if the cat was a good mouser," Darbishire agreed. "Still, I get your point, Jen. It's bound to belong to someone, though."

The more they debated the problem the more puzzling it became, and they were soon forced to the conclusion that the animal's ownership must rank as one of the great unsolved mysteries of modern times. The question of what to do next was equally puzzling.

"We can't hand it in as Lost Property if nobody's lost it,"

Darbishire argued. "And if we gave it to a master he'd just say pets aren't allowed and turn it loose to fend for itself."

This was unthinkable. A small, helpless pet should be treated with loving care and attention and protected against the dangers of a chance meeting with Matron's cat; to say nothing of the perils in store in the outside world beyond the school gates.

It was Jennings, as usual, who made the decision. "I vote we keep it," he said. "At any rate, until we find out who it really belongs to."

"But what about the rules?" protested Darbishire.

Jennings shrugged. "It'll have to be a secret pet, that's all. Nobody must know anything about it – least of all Old Wilkie, or any of the masters."

He picked up the little animal, stroked it and scratched its head with his forefinger. It seemed to enjoy this treatment, for it remained quite still in the palm of his hand and made no attempt to escape.

Jennings' eyes shone with pleasure. Only a week before his imagination had conjured up a situation such as this, but not for one moment had he allowed himself to believe that it would ever become a reality.

"We ought to give him something to eat, so he'll know we're his friends," he remarked, rummaging around in the shoelockers for the missing apple. "That's funny – it's gone. Now which gruesome specimen has eaten my apple, I'd like to know?"

"It could have been lots of people," Darbishire pointed out.

"Well, if it *was* lots of people they wouldn't have got much each. It was only a tiddly little thing, hardly bigger than those shrivelled-up prunes they give us for lunch."

There was no point in wasting time arguing about the

whereabouts of the missing fruit. The more sensible course, clearly, was to go and find fresh supplies of provender.

"There'll probably be some outside cabbage leaves in the dustbin," Jennings decided, gently depositing the guinea-pig in the wastepaper basket. "Come on, let's go and see what we can find."

"I shouldn't leave him there," Darbishire cautioned.

"Why not? He'll be happy enough. He's got quite a nice view of the shoelockers through the gaps in the wicker-work."

"I dare say, but it won't be safe. That wastepaper basket gets emptied at least three times a term, and if anyone decides to do any spring-cleaning while we're away . . ."

"It'll be all right in there for just a few minutes," Jennings broke in. "In any case, we can't take him with us in case we meet anyone."

Fortunately, the guinea-pig was a docile animal. It made no attempt to escape from the basket, but settled down comfortably amidst the toffee papers and orange peel which carpeted the bottom. For safety's sake, Jennings concealed the basket behind the furthermost shoelocker, after which he and Darbishire scampered off to the courtyard behind the kitchen where the dustbins were kept.

"We ought to think of a name for him," Jennings said, as he led the way across the lobby towards the kitchen quarters.

Darbishire obliged with a selection of names composed on the spur of the moment. "Pingo, Pongo, Pango," he said as they passed the open door of the table-tennis room. A cricket scoring book lying on the floor inspired him to add, "Stumpo, Bailey, Wicket, Batsy, Howsthato, Notoutski . . ."

"Don't talk such antiseptic eyewash, Darbi," Jennings reproved. "I don't just want a made-up name. I want a proper one. I think I'll call him F. J. Saunders."

"Why?"

"Well, why not? Why are you called 'Darbishire'?"

"Oh, that's easy. My father says that years ago our family used to be known as . . ."

This was not a good moment, Jennings decided, to discuss the history of the Darbishire family.

"We'll have to look out when we get to the kitchen yard in case Mr Wilkins sees us," he interrupted. "Anyway, what made me think of it was because he looks rather like a man I know at home."

"Who does? Mr Wilkins?"

"No, you clodpoll! The guinea-pig reminds me of this bloke I was telling you about – F. J. Saunders. At least, that's what *I* call him. In fact, nearly everyone calls him that. I've even heard the vicar talk about him as Mr Saunders."

"Why?" asked Darbishire, scenting a mystery.

"Because it's his name. Honestly, Darbi, you do ask the most asinine questions. Anyone would think you were . . ."

Jennings broke off as the tall figure of Mr Wilkins came round the bend of the corridor towards them. There was something about the searching glances he kept casting to left and right that caused a pang of uneasiness in Darbishire's mind.

Mr Wilkins passed them without a word and disappeared in the direction of the tuck-box room.

"Old Sir's on the prowl," Darbishire observed when the master was safely out of earshot. "Suppose he goes to the shoeroom and starts rummaging about in the wastepaper basket?"

"Why on earth should he?"

"He might think he heard a guinea-pig inside."

"You're crazy, Darbi. Old Wilkie doesn't even know there's a guinea-pig on the premises at all, so why should he start looking through the wastepaper basket for him?"

They continued on their way towards the kitchen quarters and so failed to observe Mr Wilkins' progress to the lower ground floor.

It so happened that the master had had no intention of extending his search to such an unlikely spot as the shoelockers. But as he was passing the door of the shoeroom he was accosted by Robinson, the odd-job man, who had just begun his daily mopping-up operations in the basement.

"Excuse me, Mr Wilkins," he said. "But there's something odd in the shoeroom."

"How do you mean, *odd*?" replied Mr Wilkins, wondering whether Robinson's fancy had been stirred by something unusual in the shape of juvenile footwear.

"Gave me quite a turn it did," replied the odd-jobber. "I heard a rustle behind the lockers – like a mouse or a rat it was; and when I looked inside the wastepaper basket, there it was, with those pink eyes staring up at me as though . . ."

But Mr Wilkins was already through the door investigating the contents of the wastepaper basket.

There was no shortage of cabbage leaves in the dustbins outside the kitchen door, and Jennings and Darbishire soon filled their pockets with sufficient vegetable matter to provide F. J. Saunders with an appetising lunch.

Carefully, they replaced the lid of the dustbin and retraced their steps through the side door into the main building. They moved with caution, having no wish to draw attention to themselves, but unfortunately Mr Carter emerged from one of the empty classrooms as they were passing the door on their way to the basement stairs.

The master would have passed them by with no more than a casual glance had it not been for their efforts to look natural. Darbishire's guilty start and Jennings' expression of wide-eyed innocence warned him that all was not as it should be.

Mr Carter gave them a searching look. To his expert eye it seemed that Jennings' blazer was bulging even more than usual.

"Tut! Just look at your pockets, Jennings!" he said in tones of patient reproach. "I've told you a dozen times not to fill them to bursting point with useless junk. It ruins the shape of your blazer."

"Yes, sir." Jennings stood with his arms close to his sides, trying to compress the tell-tale bulges.

"And yours are just as bad, Darbishire," the master went on. "What on earth have you got in them?"

Darbishire swallowed hard and looked down at his shoes. "Er – cabbage," he mumbled.

"Cabbage!" Mr Carter raised a puzzled eyebrow.

"But it's all right, sir. It's not cooked or anything like that," Darbishire assured him.

There was a short silence. Then Mr Carter said, "Come along, now, Jennings. What's going on?"

Jennings shifted uncomfortably from foot to foot. He was about to confess to his discovery in the shoeroom when Mr Carter's puzzled frown suddenly disappeared and was replaced by a smile of understanding . . . Of course! Cabbage leaves . . . The missing guinea-pig!

"Light is beginning to dawn, Jennings," he said. "Tell me, have you just seen Mr Wilkins?"

"Yes, sir. In the corridor about ten minutes ago."

The mystery resolved itself in Mr Carter's mind.

Obviously Mr Wilkins, in his search for the straying rodent, had enlisted the support of Jennings and Darbishire and sent them on a foraging expedition.

"Ah, that explains it," Mr Carter said. "But there's no need to be so secretive about it. You'd better take the cabbage to Mr Wilkins at once. I expect he's waiting for it."

Jennings could hardly believe his ears. "Take the cabbage to Mr Wilkins, sir?" he echoed in bewilderment.

"Well, of course. You're not proposing to eat it yourself, are you?"

"On no, sir. I only thought . . . that is, I didn't think . . . or rather . . ." Surely Mr Carter must be joking! Why on earth should Mr Wilkins want a pocketful of uncooked vegetable matter? It just didn't make sense.

Jennings glanced up at Mr Carter, seeking a clue to the riddle, but the master had already dismissed the matter from his mind and had begun to walk away along the corridor. In a haze of doubt Jennings turned and continued his journey in the opposite direction. Darbishire, equally puzzled, trotted at his side.

"I don't get this at all. Either Mr Carter's crazy, or Old Wilkie is," Jennings muttered in worried tones.

For some moments they debated whether Mr Carter was trying to be funny at their expense. If they obeyed his instructions literally, might they not find themselves in trouble with Mr Wilkins? They had still not come to any decision when they reached the study door.

"Bags you do it, then," said Darbishire. "Give him yours and I'll keep my pocketful for F. J. Saunders."

"Well, Mr Carter *did* say, didn't he? . . ."

"Maybe he did, but that won't stop Old Wilkie from going into a roof-level attack and ticking us off for insolence."

"No, maybe it won't, but . . ."

"Go on, I dare you to!"

That settled it. Jennings raised his hand and tapped lightly on the door. If Mr Wilkins took the joke in the wrong spirit, he told himself, then Mr Carter would just have to take the blame. It wasn't fair for masters to . . .

The door opened six inches and Mr Wilkins looked out into the corridor.

"What is it?" he asked shortly.

"Please, sir, I've brought you some . . ." Suddenly Jennings' courage failed him. What he had to say would sound grossly impertinent. "It's all right, sir. It doesn't matter," he mumbled.

"Well, go on! What have you brought me?" the master demanded impatiently.

"Nothing, sir."

"But, you silly little boy, you just told me you *had*."

"Well, sir, it was just something Mr Carter said, but perhaps he didn't really mean it or he wouldn't have said it, sir. I mean . . ."

By this time Mr Wilkins was tapping his foot with impatience to know the text of the message.

". . . you see, sir, he told me to ask you if you'd like some raw cabbage, sir," Jennings ended with a gulp.

Mr Wilkins' expression changed, but not for the worse as Jennings had feared. Instead, a smile of appreciation lit up his features as he extended his hand to take the leaves.

"Yes, I should certainly like some," he said in friendly tones. "It's just what I wanted. And you couldn't have brought it at a more opportune moment. Thank you, Jennings. Thank you very much!"

The door closed, blotting out the fantastic spectacle of

Mr Wilkins gloating over a handful of stringy cabbage leaves.

Jennings rocked on his heels and clutched at the wall for support. So Mr Carter was right after all!

"Well! What do you know!" he gasped. "Things have come to a real bish when masters shut themselves in their rooms with stacks of raw vegetables!"

"It's amazing, isn't it," Darbishire agreed. "Still, my father says there's no accounting for taste. Not that there's much taste to account for in raw cabbage, of course," he added as an afterthought.

They trotted off to the shoeroom where a further shock awaited them. The wastepaper basket no longer bore signs of animal life.

"Fossilized fish-hooks! F. J. Saunders has escaped!" Jennings cried in horror. "He must have scambled up the wickerwork and over the top."

"Start looking, quick, then!" Darbishire advised. "He hasn't had time to get very far."

But a thorough search of the shoeroom and adjoining corridors proved that the animal must have gone farther afield. And, though they continued the search in their free time for the rest of the day, they were still without a clue as to the whereabouts of their secret pet when they retired to bed that evening. For the time being, F. J. Saunders had disappeared as mysteriously as he had come.

"We won't give up hope though," Jennings said as he went upstairs to bed that evening. "I'll find him if it takes me a week. You see if I don't."

Chapter 5

The Organised Outing

For two days Jennings and Darbishire searched in vain for some sign of their secret pet, unaware that the missing animal was in Mr Wilkins' safe keeping. Moreover, it seemed likely to remain there for some time, for Mrs Atkinson, senior, was in no hurry to reclaim her property. With a sweeping, grandmotherly contempt for school rules she had written to say that she was at a loss to understand what all the fuss was about; and that, in any case, she could not manage to pay another visit to Linbury before the end of the week.

By this time Mr Wilkins had become almost reconciled to his role of animal-keeper.

"I've just been giving the creature its fodder," he informed Mr Carter as they foregathered in the staff common room to discuss the Camera Club outing arranged for the following afternoon. "By the way, I meant to thank you for sending Jennings and Darbishire on that foraging expedition the other day. It came in very handy as it happened."

Mr Carter looked puzzled. "*I* didn't send them in search of feeding stuff," he said. "Surely it was you who told them to go and find some?"

"I never said a word about it. I assumed they'd done it on your instructions."

The puzzled frown deepened on Mr Carter's brow. "This is growing mysterious, Wilkins; if neither you nor I said anything to the boys, they couldn't have known there was a guinea-pig on the premises at all. And if that was the case, why should they go to so much trouble to amass a collection of greenstuff from goodness knows where?"

Mr Wilkins shrugged. "Perhaps they were planning to hold a dormitory feast after lights out," he hazarded. "We'd better keep an eye on them, Carter, in case there's any funny business brewing."

It was thus an unlucky quirk of fate that caused Mr Wilkins to leap to the right conclusion by the wrong methods; for the banquet planned to celebrate Atkinson's return from the sick-bay did not include green vegetables on the menu.

As it happened, Mr Wilkins' brilliant deduction did not seriously affect the plans for the secret feast for the next few days were so crowded with alarming developments that, for the time being, he forgot all about his suspicions.

To begin with, there was the Camera Club expedition to Dunhambury which Mr Carter was anxious to discuss.

"I think it would be a good plan to split the photographers into two groups when we get off the bus tomorrow," he suggested. "There's an exhibition of nature photos being held at the museum which I think some of the boys would like to see; so if you'll take the museum party, I'll take the rest of the photographers round the town."

"Oh, no, thank you very much, Carter," Mr Wilkins said firmly. "We'll do it the other way round, if you don't mind. I haven't forgotten the last time I took a party of boys to Dunhambury Museum."

Mr Carter smiled to himself as he remembered the trouble that had been caused by Jennings and Darbishire presenting the curator with a rusty cartwheel which they insisted was a genuine Roman relic.

"I'm not having any more capers of that sort," Mr Wilkins went on. "So, if you don't mind, Carter, *I'll* look after the boys who don't want to visit the exhibition."

"Very well, then, that's settled." Mr Carter took a list from his pocket and ran his eye down the column of names. "There won't be many in your party, Wilkins. Venables, Temple, Rumbelow and Bromwich will be going with you. And then, of course, there'll be Jennings and Darbishire and a few others."

Mr Wilkins groaned. "Oh *no*, Carter! Not those two!"

"Extremely keen photographers, both of them."

"Yes, I dare say, but . . ." Mr Wilkins made a hasty decision. "Look here, on second thoughts I think *I'll* take the boys who want to visit the museum."

"You can't keep changing your mind, Wilkins. We must have this outing properly organised," Mr Carter remarked, as he turned to consult the bus timetable on the staff-room noticeboard. "And don't sound so worried. Nobody could possibly get into mischief, just strolling round the town taking snapshots of historic buildings. The Head wants you to show them the sixteenth-century castle walls, the seventeenth-century market cross, the eighteenth-century Town Hall . . ."

"It's more likely that some silly little boy will fall head first into the nineteenth-century horse trough, and expect me to fish him out," said Mr Wilkins.

The words were spoken in ironic jest; though could he have foreseen the future, Mr Wilkins might have agreed that total immersion in the horse trough would have been a kinder fate than that which the day held in store for him.

A chattering swarm of boys alighted from the bus in the market square of Dunhambury and lined up on the pavement in two orderly ranks. Slung round their necks, or dangling down their backs were cameras in plastic cases. Smoothly, Mr Carter divided the photographic crocodile into two sections.

"We'll meet you back here by the bus stop at half past four, Wilkins," he said to his colleague, and then turned and led his party away in the direction of the Dunhambury Museum and Art Gallery, a tall, stone building situated some distance from the town centre.

Mr Wilkins ran his eye over the group assigned to his charge.

"Come along, you boys. We'll go round by the park and then make our way towards the castle," he ordered. "Keep together now, and don't straggle."

"Please, sir," Darbishire began. "Would you like me to take a snap of you standing by the . . . ?"

"No, I would not, Darbishire. Just find a partner to walk with. It's time we were moving."

"May we stop when we see something we want to photograph, sir?" Venables inquired.

Mr Wilkins nodded a grudging assent. "So long as you don't take all day over it. I don't want people lagging half a mile behind."

He set off at a lively pace towards the Dunhambury Memorial Park, a well-ordered oasis of prim lawns and tidy flowerbeds flourishing in a desert of warehouses and builders' yards about half a mile from the main thoroughfare of the town. Behind him trotted the members of the Camera Club.

To begin with, they kept closely on the heels of their leader, but as they left the High Street and turned into the road skirting the park railings they began to spread out, as first one and then another paused to take a photograph of

46

some object or building which had attracted his attention.

Jennings and Darbishire ambled along happily at the tail of the straggling crocodile. For the first time in two days they had forgotten to worry about their missing guinea-pig and were determined to enjoy every minute of the afternoon's activities.

"What sort of photos do you think we ought to take?" Darbishire asked, swinging his camera case to and fro on its strap like a fast-moving pendulum. He had only recently acquired his camera and he looked to Jennings, as a photographer of more experience, to give him some sound advice.

"Perhaps we could get some nature photos – birds and animals and that sort of thing," said Jennings hopefully. "Or if not, there'll be plenty of old ruins and ancient relics when we get to the castle walls."

"I'd like to take a snap of Old Wilkie, if he'll let me."

"He's not an ancient relic," Jennings pointed out. "Well, I suppose he *is*, in a way. But it's a waste of good film taking photos of masters. I took one of Mr Carter talking to the Head outside the gym last term, only he moved at the wrong moment and all I got was the bald spot on the top of his head."

"Mr Carter hasn't got a bald spot."

"I mean the Head's head. *La* cranium of ye Archbeako," Jennings explained. "It turned out such a gruesome snapshot that I didn't dare show . . ."

His voice died away and he stopped in his tracks. Beyond the green park railings on his right, he had just caught sight of a grey squirrel reared up on its hind-legs and darting quick, eager glances from side to side. By chance it had come to rest in front of one of the warning notices dotted about the lawns of the park. *Keep off the Grass*, the sign proclaimed.

Here was a scene well worth the attention of a skilled photographer, Jennings decided. It had, moreover, an air of comedy which appealed to him strongly, for if the picture came out as he hoped, it would show a cheeky squirrel cheerfully flouting the bye-laws of the Dunhambury Borough Council. The utmost stealth must be observed if the photograph was to be a success.

"Ssh, Darbi! Ssh!" he breathed. "Don't move! Don't even bat an eyelid."

"I wasn't moving; my eyelids weren't batting," Darbishire said loudly. "What's up, anyway?"

"Quiet! Over there in the park, look. There's a squirrel reading a noticeboard just the other side of the railings."

Darbishire peered in the direction of his friend's pointing finger.

"Wow! So there is!" he exclaimed excitedly. "Take a photo, quick, Jen. It'll make a snappersonic soupshot!"

"A *what*?"

"A supersonic snapshot," Darbishire corrected as Jennings whipped his camera out of its case and levelled it at the squirrel beyond the railings.

"Tut! There's something wrong with this gadget," Jennings complained. "I can't see a thing through the viewfinder."

"You've got your finger over the front," Darbishire whispered.

"Eh? Oh, yes, so I have."

With this obstruction removed, Jennings could see the squirrel quite clearly. The only trouble was that he could see the park railings as well which, in a photograph, would give the impression that the animal was behind the bars of

48

a cage. This effect completely spoilt the illusion that he was hoping to create, so he crept forward across the pavement and pushed the camera through the railings and held it with his hands inserted between the bars on either side.

It was then that he found himself beset by a further difficulty. True, the railings were no longer in the way; but as the camera was on one side of them and Jennings was on the other, he was unable to bend his head forward to look into the viewfinder.

"Poke your head through the railings," Darbishire advised. "There's just about enough room. Only hurry up about it: the squirrel won't stop there all day waiting for you."

Clearly there was no time to be lost and the keen photographer acted on the advice without delay. The feat was not easy to perform because the space between the bars was almost identical with the width of Jennings' head, but after some strenuous wriggling he achieved his object at the expense of two badly chafed ears.

The next moment there came the click of the camera shutter; the squirrel, startled by the sound, scampered away to the nearest tree.

"Did you get it?" Darbishire asked anxiously.

"Yes. I could see it *bang-slap* in the middle of the viewfinder," Jennings answered. "It should make a perfect nature photo."

Darbishire glanced along the road and noticed that Mr Wilkins and the main body of photographers were now some distance ahead, climbing the slope which led to the castle walls.

"Come on, then, we'd better catch up with the others," he said. "Old Wilkie will go berserk if we get too far behind."

"Yes, I know, we'll have to get a move on if we're going to . . . *Ouch!*"

Jennings broke off with a sudden yelp of anguish as he attempted to withdraw his head through the railings. He tried again, cautiously at first, and then tugged and strained with increasing force as the terrible truth dawned on him . . . *He was stuck!*

Panic seized him. "Help! Help! Get me out!" he wailed.

"Oh come on, Jen; don't muck about," urged Darbishire, anxious to be on his way.

"I'm not . . . mucking about . . . honestly, Darbi."

"What are you playing at then?"

"I can't get my head back through the railings."

"What!"

Darbishire's eyes opened wide in horror as the full meaning of the frantic contortions dawned on him. "Petrified fish-hooks! Oh, my goodness! Are you sure? Pull harder!"

"Ow . . . Ouch . . . It's no good pulling harder. It just won't come."

"It went through easily enough," Darbishire pointed out unhelpfully. "It must be your ears; they stick out too much. I've always said your ears remind me of the silver sports cup in the library."

"Wow! Oh, help, this is frantic!" moaned the unhappy prisoner. Tears welled up in his eyes. Wriggle and writhe as he might, he knew now that he could not set himself free by his own efforts.

"Not the junior football cup, of course," continued Darbishire, anxious to make his meaning quite clear. "I mean the other one on the mantelpiece with big handles sticking out each side at right angles."

"Oh, for goodness' sake, Darbi!" Jennings cried in

50

exasperation. "Don't just stand there telling me which silver sports cup my ears remind you of. *Do* something!"

"Yes, all right. I'll – er – I'll hold the camera for you, shall I?"

"A fat lot of good that'll do. Do something to get my head out, you addle-pated clodpoll!"

Darbishire searched his mind for some way out of the crisis. He could not bend the bars apart like a strong man at a circus, but neither could he allow his friend to remain for ever in his present position.

There was only one thing to be done and this, in itself, was likely to lead to further trouble . . . But C. E. J. Darbishire did not flinch from his unpleasant decision.

"I shall have to call Old Wilkie," he said uneasily.

Mr Wilkins was halfway up the hill to the castle ruins when the cries of distress rang out behind him. He turned and saw an agitated figure waving its arms like windmill sails and pointing to a companion who appeared to be admiring the scenery on the far side of the park railings.

It was impossible, at that distance, to distinguish the features of the boys, but Mr Wilkins had little difficulty in guessing which two members of his flock were disturbing the orderly calm that had so far prevailed.

"Tut! Silly little boys!" he muttered, and beckoned to them to stop playing about and catch up with the rest of the party.

His signals were ignored. Instead of obeying instructions the cavorting figure on the pavement danced even more wildly, uttering hoarse shouts and making frantic gestures of woe.

"I think he wants you to go back, sir," said Temple who, with Venables and Bromwich, had been walking alongside Mr Wilkins as they climbed the hill.

"Aren't you going back to see, sir? Perhaps it's urgent," suggested Bromwich.

"Yes, I *am* going. And what's more, it had *better* be urgent," said Mr Wilkins shortly. If those silly little boys expected him to go all the way back to the bottom of the hill merely to be asked his opinion on some trivial detail of photography, he was prepared to express his feelings very tersely indeed.

Most of the group had now reached the top of the slope, so Mr Wilkins sent Bromwich up to join them with orders that they were to wait by the castle ruins until further notice. Then, frowning and muttering with annoyance, he turned and retraced his steps down the hill. At a safe distance behind him came Temple and Venables, hoping for trouble and anxious not to miss any excitement that might be laid on for their entertainment.

Mr Wilkins still had no clue as to why he had been summoned when he came within hailing distance of the boys by the railings. All he could judge was that Darbishire appeared to have gone mad, while Jennings was taking far longer than necessary over his snapshot of some object inside the park.

"Come along, you boys, come along!" Mr Wilkins boomed angrily as he strode up to them. "What on earth are you playing at? I distinctly told you not to lag behind."

"Something rather awkward has happened, sir," Darbishire volunteered. "You see, Jennings was taking a photo and . . ."

Mr Wilkins glanced at the motionless figure. "Jennings! Stop peering through those railings and catch up at once. You've had time to take fifty photographs!"

Somewhat to Mr Wilkins' surprise, Jennings did not look

round when spoken to. Unhappily, he quavered, "I can't come, sir. I can't get my head back."

"Eh! Of all the ridiculous tomfoolery!"

"It's his ears, sir," Darbishire explained. "They're like the handles on the sports cup in the library, sir. Not the junior football cup, of course; I mean the one on the mantelpiece standing next to the . . ."

"*Doh! I – I – corwumph!*" Mr Wilkins broke in. "What did you want to poke your head through for, you silly little boy?"

"I saw a squirrel, sir."

"Saw a squirrel!"

"Yes, sir. A grey one, sir."

"What in the name of thunder has that got to do with it?" Mr Wilkins demanded irritably. "Civilised people don't rush up to the nearest iron railings and stick their heads through every time they see a squirrel!"

By this time Venables and Temple had edged close enough to take a lively interest in the proceedings.

"I don't quite see how it happened," Temple queried. "If his head went through one way, it ought to come back again."

"Ah, not with those right-angled ear-flaps of his," replied Darbishire knowingly. "I'll show you how it happened, shall I? He put his hands through the railings, like this, to hold his camera, and then he poked his head through the gap in the middle . . ."

Out of the corner of his eye Mr Wilkins caught sight of Darbishire's demonstration. The prospect of having to rescue two wedged heads instead of one caused him to burst out in alarm, "No, no, no, Darbishire! Stop it! Stop it at once! It's bad enough having one foolish youth stuck fast without you joining in for the fun of the thing!"

"Sorry, sir," Darbishire apologised as he withdrew from the danger area. "I was only going to demonstrate my famous theory of one-way, non-return ear-flaps."

Loud tut-tuts of exasperation broke on the air as Mr Wilkins bent to his task of freeing the unhappy prisoner. Gingerly, he tried to ease the chafed ears through the bars, but his efforts met with no success.

"Come along, now, Jennings," he urged. "You'll have to get your head back somehow or other."

"But I can't, sir. I've been trying all the time," Jennings protested as he made further vain efforts to free himself. "I think my head must have swelled, or the gap must have shrunk, or something, sir."

"This is ridiculous!" fumed Mr Wilkins, pausing for breath. "You really are a silly little boy, Jennings!"

"Yes, sir. I know, sir."

Action, prompt and immediate was Mr Wilkins' watchword. With his bare hands he could do nothing: the situation called for tools and special equipment to force the bars apart. He must send for help without delay. Surely the fire brigade would have some gadget for freeing people foolish enough to stick their heads between iron railings!

"I am going to summon assistance," he announced.

"You may need help, sir," Temple suggested. "I mean, you may need someone to assist you to summon help, sir."

"Very well, then. You can come with me, Temple. We'll go and find a phone box at once," Mr Wilkins decided. Somewhat unnecessarily, he added, "And you stay where you are, Jennings. Don't move till I get back."

Without more ado, the master, with Temple at his side, turned and hurried off towards the town centre on his errand of liberation.

Chapter 6

Darbishire to the Rescue

Darbishire and Venables spent the first few minutes after Mr Wilkins' departure in sympathising with the unhappy prisoner and taking photographs of him from various angles.

"Can't you manage to screw your head round just a little bit more, Jen?" Venables urged, as he frowned into his viewfinder. "I've only got one exposure left, and I'd like to take a nice smiling one of you to end up with."

"Huh! I'd like to see *you* smiling in my place," Jennings grumbled.

"Try saying 'cheese' then. From where I'm standing you look like one of those blokes in the pillory that Old Wilkie was telling us about in history. Some of those characters had to stand there for ever so long and everybody used to gather round and throw . . ."

"All right, all right. I don't want to hear about it."

"I was only trying to cheer you up," Venables went on chattily. "After all, I don't see what you've got to moan about. Old Wilkie will be back soon, and in the meantime you've got quite a nice view of the park through that gap in the rhododendrons."

The captive snorted. "A fine time to tell me to admire the scenery!"

Soon, however, the novelty of comforting the prisoner and making a visual record of his plight began to pall.

"I wonder how long Old Wilkie will be?" queried Darbishire, glancing at his watch. "Let's go along to the corner and see if we can see him coming back."

"Come on, then," Venables agreed, starting off down the road at a fast trot.

A wail of protest rang out from behind him. "Hey, stop! Don't go away and leave me!" Jennings pleaded.

"We're only going to the corner. We'll be back in a sec," Darbishire assured him. "It's all for your good, really, because we shall be able to tell you if there's any sign of help coming along."

But as it happened there was no trace of Mr Wilkins and the long-awaited help, when Darbishire and Venables reached the corner where the park road crossed an avenue of semi-detached houses. Few people were about, and the only vehicle in sight was a car parked in the avenue a few yards from the crossroads.

The car was an old-fashioned model with dented wings and streaks of rust showing through the paintwork.

Darbishire stood staring at the vehicle in a trance of concentration, while a Bright Idea blossomed in his brain. Suddenly, he smote himself on the forehead and turned to his companion with eyes shining in triumph behind his dusty spectacles.

"Crystallized cheesecakes! I've got it!" he cried. "A brainwave, if ever there was one!"

Venables looked blank. "Uh?" he queried.

"That ancient old crock of a car over there," Darbishire went on, flinging out a hand in the direction of the dilapidated vehicle. "If we borrowed the jack from its tool-kit, we might be able to get Jennings free without waiting for Old Wilkie."

Venables was slow in grasping the gist of Darbishire's

brainwave. He maintained that no good would come of jacking Jennings up clear of the ground as though he were the back axle of a car, and that Darbishire was talking through his size six-and-three-quarters headgear in proposing such a bat-witted suggestion.

"Who said anything about lifting him off the ground?" Darbishire demanded. "My plan is to use the jack to bend the bars outwards, you clodpoll."

There was much to be said for the *Darbishire Method of Removing Heads from Railings*, as the inventor proudly styled his scheme. All you had to do was to turn the jack on its side and insert it between the bars just above the head of the unfortunate victim. Then, by turning the handle, the jack could be screwed in a horizontal direction to exert a sideways pressure on the railings.

"Yes, of course. Really lobsterous idea!" Venables agreed when the method had been explained to him. "Fancy you thinking out a treatment like that. You must have supercharged electronic brain cells!"

The inventor breathed on his fingernails and polished them on the lapel of his raincoat. "It came to me in a flash," he said airily. "I often get strokes of genius. Some people do, you know."

"Well, you needn't boast about it till we know if it works," his companion retorted. "Come on, let's go across and ask if we can borrow the jack."

Unfortunately the car was unattended, and though the boys looked up and down the road there was no sign of the driver.

"I expect he's just parked it and gone off," Venables hazarded. "Let's have a look in the tool-kit and see if he's got a jack."

He jerked open the unlocked boot and rummaged

amongst the tools. Then, with a cry of triumph, he lifted out a rusty car jack and a metal bar which served as its handle. He set them down noisily on the pavement.

"There we are. Just the job! I can hardly wait to try out your famous plan, Darbi."

In its closed position, the jack was about six inches in length which, as Darbishire pointed out, was roughly the width of Jennings' head, not counting his ears. With any luck the tool would fit snugly in the gap between the railings . . .

So far so good. But what would happen if they made off with the equipment without the owner's consent?

"I don't like taking it without per," Darbishire muttered in worried tones.

"Why not? We're going to bring it back in a couple of minutes, aren't we? We shan't do it any harm."

"I dare say, but my father says you should never . . ."

"Oh, don't talk such antiseptic eyewash, Darbishire," interrupted Venables, whose concern over Jennings' plight was now somewhat less than his curiosity to know whether Darbishire's experiment would really work. "The owner couldn't possibly object. I bet you what you like he'd be only too pleased to lend it if he knew what we wanted it for!"

"M'yes. After all, it *is* an emergency," Darbishire reasoned. "And we can ask per when we bring it back, if he's here."

"And if he isn't, he won't know anything about it, so he won't mind anyway."

Venables slammed down the lid of the boot, picked up the jack and hurried back towards the park. Darbishire followed, twirling the jack handle before him like a drum major leading a military band.

Jennings had grown tired of the view of the park through the rhododendron bushes by the time his companions returned.

"Where have you two gruesome specimens been?" he demanded. "You are a couple of weeds pushing off like that."

"It's all right, Jen. I've had a brainwave," Darbishire consoled him. "Look what I've brought."

"How *can* I look! I haven't got eyes in the back of my head."

"Sorry, I was forgetting. It's a famous invention of mine. Just keep still while Venables and I give you the treatment."

Venables held the car jack in position above Jennings' head, while Darbishire turned the handle. After a few turns of the screw the tool was gripped between the railings, but the task of bending the bars outwards was more than Darbishire could manage by himself.

"Phew! This isn't going to be easy," he panted. "Leave your end, Ven, and come and help me on the handle."

The two boys heaved and strained and gradually their efforts were rewarded.

"It's bending! I can see it!" Venables shouted excitedly. "Another quarter of an inch should do it . . . Try again now, Jennings."

The prisoner renewed his efforts and, as the bars yielded to the pressure, he found himself able to wriggle clear of their grip.

He was free! He stood upright, uttered a wild yell of triumph, and backed across the pavement exulting in his new-found liberty.

"Hurray! Terrific! We've done it!" he crowed as his liberators stopped work and joined him in an ungainly ballet dance up and down the road.

"Good old Darbi and Venables!" Jennings chanted as he danced. "Well done, you two. Hearty congrats and many thanks. I don't know where you get all these famous ideas from, Darbi. No one would think you had the brains of a shrimp, to look at you."

"Oh, it's just a flair I've got," the inventor explained as the dance came to an end. "My father says some people are . . ."

"Never mind about that," Venables broke in. "We'd better take ye famous tool back to the car now we've finished with it."

"Yes, of course," Darbishire agreed. "And you'd better come too, Jen, in case the driver's there and wants to know what's been going on. Just show him how your ears stick out and he'll soon see why we needed special equipment to get you unwedged."

They dismantled the car jack and inspected the railings for signs of damage. Fortunately this was so slight that it was barely perceptible, for it had not been necessary to bend the bars more than half an inch in either direction.

"Old Wilkie ought to be really pleased, anyway," Venables observed. "We've fixed up everything nicely without bothering him at all."

Darbishire glowed with quiet pride. "We'll just return ye famous life-saving implement and then come straight back and wait for him," he said as he picked up the jack from the pavement.

"Like me to carry it for you?" Jennings offered.

"No fear. After all, it was my method, so bags I carry the tools."

The car was still parked by the kerb when they reached the end of the road. As they turned the corner, they were just in time to see an elderly man in a battered felt hat and fawn coat climbing into the driver's seat.

"Goodo. The bloke's come back. Now we can ask his per," said Darbishire, quickening his pace.

"It's a bit late to do that," Jennings observed as the engine gave an asthmatic cough and leapt to life.

"Well, we can explain why we wanted it."

"It's a bit late to do that, too. He's just . . ." Jennings broke off, for at that moment there came a cloud of blue smoke from the exhaust pipe and the car started off down the road at an unsteady fifteen kph.

Panic and dismay seized the group.

"Fossilized fish-hooks! Hey! Hi! Whoa! Come back!" shouted Darbishire.

"Stop, stop! You've gone without your tools!" shrilled Venables.

Their shouts were drowned by the squawks of an ear-splitting gear change as the car moved away from them at increasing speed.

"Crystallized cheesecakes! What are we going to do now?" wailed Darbishire. "We've got to give the thing back to him somehow. We can't keep it."

"After him, quick!" Jennings commanded, breaking into a run.

"What, on foot! But we'll never catch him up. We can't run as fast as a car!"

"He may stop at a traffic light, or something," Jennings called back over his shoulder. "Come on, you lot, *run* for goodness' sake. We've got to catch him *somehow*."

Venables sprinted after Jennings, leaving Darbishire to bring up the rear. Nature had never intended Darbishire to be a four-minute miler. Now, bowed down by the weight of the jack and impeded by the handle which kept swinging between his knees, it was as much as he could do, after the first thirty seconds of the pursuit, to keep his fellow runners in sight.

"Oh, fish-hooks, why did I say I'd carry the beastly thing?" he mumbled to himself as he tottered along in the wake of his colleagues.

For a hundred yards the road ran straight and Jennings was able to keep the green car in sight. Then came a sharp curve and the car disappeared from view.

Jennings ran on with dwindling hopes. There was just a chance that he would catch another glimpse of his quarry if he ran his fastest, for he knew that once round the bend the road was straight again for some little distance. Even so, he could not keep up his present pace for long. Everything depended on whether, by some lucky chance, the motorist would stop within the next quarter of a mile.

Panting and breathless, Jennings bounded up to the bend. The car was still ahead, though it was fast becoming a mere speck on the horizon. As he watched it, it turned off down a side road on the right, and he set off once more in pursuit.

This time his luck was out, for when he reached the side road the car had vanished. There was nothing he could do except wait for the others to catch up.

A few moments later Venables came panting along to join him; and considerably later still a sound like a farm lorry wheezing up a steep gradient announced that C. E. J. Darbishire was once more amongst those present.

"This is hopeless," Venables complained, when he had recovered his breath. "We've come all this way and now we've lost him."

"We'll have to press on all the same," Jennings urged. "Let's go down this road and see if there's any sign of him round the next corner. Come on, Darbi, let's get going."

"Come on!" echoed Darbishire, scarlet in the face with exertion. "I like the cheek of that! You make me carry this massive great jack weighing about a hundred tons and then expect me to go bursting through the sound barrier!"

"That's your bad luck! I offered to carry it and you wouldn't let me," Jennings pointed out.

"You can carry it now, if you want to."

"No fear! You bagged it. You can't volunteer for an important job like that and then back out in the middle."

"Ah, but how was I to know this was going to happen?" Darbishire defended himself. "And anyway, it's all thanks to you. If you hadn't been such a petrified clodpoll as to stick your great head through the railings, we shouldn't be in this jam now."

"Hear, hear," said Venables. "I vote we call the whole thing off."

Jennings was shocked by this irresponsible suggestion.

"We can't give up yet," he protested warmly. "What are we going to do with the thing? If we hang on to it we shall probably be arrested for taking it without permish or something ghastly."

"Couldn't we send it back by post?"

"Don't be crazy. We don't know where to send it. We don't even know the number of the car, so we'll just *have* to go on searching."

Darbishire blew out his cheeks and glowered at his companions in disgust. It was really unfair, he told himself, that his brilliant brainwave which should, by rights, be the sole topic of conversation, had given place to this futile debate. As the inventor of the *Darbishire Method of Removing Heads from Railings* he should, at this moment, be basking in glory and smiling modestly at the congratulations of his colleagues: instead of which, weighed down with equipment and drooping with fatigue, he found himself obliged to lumber past rows of semi-detached villas in search of a missing motorist. It was really unfair!

He was about to draw attention to this injustice when Venables suddenly exclaimed, "Petrified cheesecakes! What about Old Wilkie? He may be back by now and he'll be wondering what's happened to us."

Events had moved so quickly since the master's departure that they had forgotten all about his instructions until this moment.

"One of us ought to go back and see if he's there," Jennings decided. "I'll tell you what. You and Darbi go on searching up and down these side roads in case the car's still somewhere around these parts, while I nip back to the park and tell old Wilkie what's happened."

"Well, don't be long about it," Venables warned him. "If we haven't found it by the time you get back, I vote we go straight to the nearest police station and hand the jack over to them."

"Don't worry," Jennings assured him as they parted on the corner. "Old Wilkie will know what to do . . . After all, he's in charge of this outing, so it's up to him to cope with the hoo-hah, isn't it?"

Chapter 7

Emergency Call

It took Mr Wilkins far longer than he had expected to summon aid for Jennings' release. The first telephone kiosk that he came across was occupied by a talkative lady engaged in a conversation which seemed likely to last for the rest of the afternoon.

He tapped on the glass panels of the kiosk and waved his hands in lively dumb show to indicate the urgency of his mission. His signals were ignored. The chatty caller turned her back on him and refused to open the door.

With Temple skipping excitedly at his heels, Mr Wilkins hurried away in search of another kiosk.

Again their luck was out. The next call box they found was labelled "Out of Order" and by the time they arrived at a third, some distance away from the park, Mr Wilkins had lost the cool, calm and collected frame of mind so essential for the smooth handling of awkward crises.

Breathless and flurried, he hurled open the door, snatched the receiver from its rest and poured out a torrent of directions. Then he remembered that he had not yet called the exchange. With a grunt of annoyance he dialled "999" and drummed his fingers impatiently on the coin box as he waited for the exchange to answer.

Outside on the pavement, Temple pressed his nose to the glass door panel and listened to one side of the conversation that came from within.

"Hallo! Hallo! Is that the Operator? Can you hear me? This is urgent!" he heard Mr Wilkins boom into the mouthpiece. Some query must have been raised at the other end, for after a pause he went on, "No, no, no, not *Mr* Urgent! My name's Wilkins . . . Yes, I know I said it was urgent. So it is. It's an emergency! Fire, Police, Ambulance – whichever one has a gadget for setting people free when they're stuck. You see, I'm in a phone box not far from the park, and . . . No, no, no, *I*'m not stuck in a phone box – it's a boy I'm in charge of. He's parked his head between the railings – I – I mean, he's stuck it between the park railings!"

Anxious to be of assistance, Temple opened the door and said, "Is everything all right, sir? Anything I can do?"

"Be quiet, and don't interrupt. I don't want any help from you!" Mr Wilkins barked testily.

Apparently this remark was not well received at the other end of the line, for he burst into a further flurry of explanations.

"No, no, I'm not talking to *you*, operator! I was just speaking to a boy who poked his head through the door. Not the same boy – a different one. The other boy poked his head through the railings and I want you to put me through to the proper authority at once!"

In a matter of seconds Mr Wilkins' call had been transferred to the watch room of the Dunhambury Fire Station. To his annoyance, he found himself obliged to explain the situation all over again.

"Hullo! Fire Station? My name's Wilkins, and it's urgent!" he began. "*Spell* it? U—R—G—E—N— . . . I mean, W—I—L—K—I—N—S. I want you to bring the gadget you use for releasing heads parked between wedged railings – I mean, wedged between park railings. One of my

66

boys has got himself in rather a tangle at the bottom of the hill leading up to the castle . . ."

Flushed with agitation and short of temper, Mr Wilkins bustled out of the telephone box and seized Temple by the arm.

"Come along, boy. Hurry up, and don't dawdle. I want to get back to Jennings before the fire brigade arrives."

"Yes, rather, sir. Terrific fun, isn't it?" said Temple, trotting along by the master's side.

"It's nothing of the sort! It's infuriating! Quickly, now! Can't you go any faster? The fire-engine will be there before we are, at this rate, and I must be on hand to explain matters to the officer in charge."

In silence they hurried back to the park, though it was as much as Temple could do to stem the flow of happy prattle which rose to his lips. He was enjoying himself immensely. The afternoon's programme was proving even more entertaining than he had expected. The photographic expedition was, of course, a treat in itself. Jennings' mishap had added to the general gaiety in what Temple considered to be a most satisfactory manner . . . And as if that were not enough, there was the prospect of being on hand to witness the supreme thrill of all – fire-engines racing pell-mell through the quiet streets: wailing sirens shattering the peaceful stillness of the afternoon! . . . This, thanks to Jennings, was an outing that he would long remember.

"We're nearly there now, sir. We'll be able to see him from this corner," he panted breathlessly.

Tingling with excitement, he ran ahead and sprinted the last few yards from the corner, anxious to relay the latest news to the prisoner and his waiting colleagues.

"Hey, you guys! What do you think?" he burst out as he rounded the bend. And then he stopped dead and stared wide-eyed along the empty road leading up to the castle ruins.

His eyes were still round with wonder when Mr Wilkins joined him a few seconds later.

"He's not there, sir! He's gone! They've all gone, sir! Venables and Darbishire too, sir!" Temple blurted out in shocked surprise.

Mr Wilkins' jaw dropped slightly. The boy was right! What on earth could have happened?

"Perhaps we've come to the wrong part of the park, sir."

"Don't be ridiculous! This is where we left him, and this is where I told the fire brigade to come."

At that moment the wail of a fire siren broke on the air, and a gleaming red appliance rounded the corner. Mr Wilkins leaped like a mountain goat and clutched at the park railings for support.

What could he say to explain matters? . . . How could he justify his action in calling the brigade if there was no one for them to rescue?

Temple hopped from foot to foot in wild excitement. "Here they come! Goodo!" he shrilled. "Three rousing cheers for our brave firemen! Hip, hip, hooray!"

The appliance drew up beside the kerb; the leading-fireman jumped down and trotted smartly up to Mr Wilkins.

" onder if you could help me," he said in brisk tones. "W . e had a special service call to the park, but we seem to have come to the wrong spot."

"No, no, you're perfectly correct. This is the place right enough," Mr Wilkins replied uneasily.

The leading-fireman looked up and down the road. "I don't see how it can be. The message said there was a lad here in a spot of trouble."

"Yes, there is – *was* . . . It was I who sent for you."

"Ah, now we're getting somewhere. If you're the man who called us out, perhaps you'll show us where he is."

Mr Wilkins swallowed hard and twisted his fingers in embarrassment.

"I – I don't know. I can't understand it," he said blankly. "He must be somewhere about. He can't possibly be anywhere else."

It was not a convincing answer and Mr Wilkins became aware that the fireman was eyeing him with deep suspicion. Confused now, he floundered on, "It's most extraordinary. He was here a few minutes ago, wedged as firm as a rock, and now he's gone . . . Vanished! Disappeared!"

The look of suspicion deepened on the fireman's face. He shot a quick glance at Temple and asked, "What about this lad? Are you sure it's not *him* you're looking for?"

"Of course I'm sure. He's been with me all the time. I tell you there was another boy: I left him here with two others – three boys altogether."

"All with their heads stuck in the railings?"

"No, no! Only one of them was stuck. And even *he's* gone now. I tell you the whole thing's uncannibal – er – uncanny – incredible!"

"What you mean is, you've called us out for nothing." The leading-fireman wagged a large forefinger at Mr Wilkins. "Are you sure this lad ever existed, because if this is a false alarm . . ."

"Good heavens no! It isn't a false alarm; it's a genuine emergency," the master protested. "This is an organised outing. I'm in charge of a school party."

"Funny sort of caper to organise on an outing!"

"You don't understand . . ."

"I understand one thing well enough, mate." The large forefinger wagged more vigorously and gave Mr Wilkins an accusing prod on the chest. "You call us out with some cock-and-bull story to rescue someone who vanishes like a puff of smoke as soon as we get here. If that's not a false alarm I should like to know what is! I shall have to put in a report about this, you know."

"Yes, yes, yes. But I can explain . . . Or rather, I can't explain . . ." Mr Wilkins broke off with a shrug.

"I know your sort! Wanted to see the fire-engine dashing along, eh? Tut-tut! And at *your* age, too!"

Shaking his head in reproof, the leading-fireman turned back towards the appliance parked by the kerb. "We'll be getting back to the station. Our officer takes a serious view of us being called out on wild goose chases, you know."

"But I assure you . . ."

"All right, Charlie, start her up. Another false alarm."

There came the bark of the self-starter, the engine leapt to life and the appliance reversed across the road, swung round and drove away towards the centre of the town. Pink to the ears with mortification, Mr Wilkins watched it go. As it turned the corner he mopped his brow and heaved a sigh of exasperation.

"Most embarrassing!" he muttered. "I wouldn't have had this happen for anything. Why couldn't the silly little boy have stayed where he was!"

"Stayed where he was, sir?" Temple echoed in surprise. "But I thought you *wanted* him to get free."

"Of course I wanted him to get free, but . . . Oh, be quiet, Temple, you infuriating child!" Mr Wilkins fumed. "Just wait till I see Master Jennings again, that's all. Just wait!"

His wish was granted sooner than he expected, for even

as he spoke a slim figure in a fawn raincoat came into view round the corner.

"*Jennings!*"

The word forced its way through Mr Wilkins' vocal chords in a strangled squawk. "I – I – I! Come here, boy. Come here at once!"

Camera in hand, Jennings approached.

"Yes, sir?"

"What – what – what, in the name of thunder, have you been doing?"

"Just now, do you mean, sir?" Jennings inquired, fumbling to replace his camera in the case hanging from his shoulder. "I was just taking a photograph of the fire-engine, sir." He fastened the strap and asked eagerly, "Did you see the fire-engine, sir? It was one of those new ones."

Mr Wilkins appeared to be in the grip of some powerful emotion. He clasped his hands to his head and marked time upon the pavement as though taking part in some primitive tribal war dance.

"Did I see the fire-engine! Did *I* see the fire-engine!" he spluttered. "I – I – I – *Doh*! I should think I *did* see the fire-engine, you silly little boy!"

"I only wondered, sir," said Jennings, taking a step backwards from the irate war-dancer.

"All the trouble I went to and you hadn't got the sense to . . . How did you get free?"

"Darbishire let me out with a car jack, sir."

"Oh, he did, did he?!"

"Yes, sir. But unfortunately the car's disappeared and we can't find it to give the jack back, sir."

By the time he had heard the details of the *Darbishire Method of Removing Heads from Railings*, Mr Wilkins' expression was a mask of disapproval. He had no word of praise for Darbishire's genius. Instead, he was very angry indeed to think that the boys had taken matters into their own hands!

He had spent a nerve-racking five minutes trying to allay the suspicions of the fire brigade. That had been bad enough. But now it seemed that he would have to pacify an enraged motorist whose tools had been borrowed without his knowledge or consent. Was there no limit to the stupidity of these silly little boys? he asked himself bitterly. It was infuriating! Why couldn't they leave things in the capable hands of the master in charge?

Clearly, the first thing to be done was to find Venables and Darbishire and stop them from making matters even worse than they were already. Goodness knows what might happen if they were entrusted with the task of explaining matters to the owner of the car jack – even supposing that he could be found!

In the worry and fuss of the last half hour, Mr Wilkins had been unable to spare a thought for the rest of his party whom he had left to their own devices in the castle ruins. But as he was about to set forth in search of the two absentees, a hubbub of voices and the clatter of juvenile footwear descending the hill warned him that the rest of his flock had grown tired of waiting and were reporting for further instructions.

"What's going on, sir? We've been waiting hours and hours!" Bromwich announced in pained tones as the group arrived at the bottom of the hill.

"Yes, sir, we saw you talking to a fire-engine, but we couldn't see anything burning, sir," volunteered Blotwell. "We wondered if there was anything on fire."

Temple was tempted to say that the only thing likely to have gone up in smoke was the master in charge of the expedition, but one glance at Mr Wilkins' smouldering expression warned him to reserve this comment until the master was out of earshot.

"I'm too busy to bother about you boys at the moment," Mr Wilkins said. "You'd better go back to the castle and take some more photographs."

At once there was a loud chorus of protest.

"Oh, sir! Not *again*, sir! We've been there about a hundred years already, honestly, sir," complained Binns.

"Yes, sir, and we've taken millions of photos," added Rumbelow. "I took one of Binns storming the ramparts with a water-pistol, and he took one of me defending the tower singlehanded against the enemy. And Martin-Jones took one of Thompson pretending to swim the moat . . ."

"All right, all right, that's enough!" Interesting though the subject was, Mr Wilkins had no intention of listening to a long-winded account of the afternoon's photographic activities. He must lose no time in tracing the missing car, a task which would be simpler to achieve without the assistance of Messrs Binns, Blotwell and Co. Unfortunately he would have to take Jennings with him, for otherwise he might be unable to find Venables and Darbishire.

"All you boys, except Jennings, go back to the bus stop and wait for me there," the master ordered. "You take charge, Bromwich, and see they behave themselves on the way."

"Yes, sir."

"Oh, but sir, can't I come with you, sir?" Temple implored.

"No, you certainly can't!"

"Oh, but sir!" A frown of disappointment furrowed Temple's brow as he joined the jostling crocodile of boys lining up on the pavement. Considering all the trouble he had taken in his role of right-hand man to Mr Wilkins, it was most unfair that his help should be spurned now that matters were again coming to a head.

"Mouldy chizz!" he complained to his partner as the crocodile began to move away towards the town centre. "Just like Old Wilkie to go and bish up the issue . . . It's absolutely not fair!"

Chapter 8

Jack Carr's Car Jack

Few people were about as Jennings led Mr Wilkins back to the meeting place he had arranged with Darbishire and Venables. The sun had disappeared behind the clouds and the blustery March wind blowing in their faces chilled Mr Wilkins' spirits to absolute zero.

It was hardly surprising that he did not relish the task which lay ahead. He had not yet regained his composure after his embarrassing encounter with the Dunhambury Fire Brigade: and now, with his nerves frayed and his temper ruffled, he was expected to cope with an even more delicate situation.

How should he try to explain matters to the owner of the car jack? What should he do if the elusive motorist could not be found? On one point only was his mind fully made up. Never again would he offer to take charge of an organised outing in which J. C. T. Jennings was included as a member of the party.

At that moment, Mr Wilkins' train of thought was broken by the sound of running footsteps. Looking up, he saw Venables racing along the road to meet him and followed, some distance behind, by Darbishire, his speed reduced to a crawl by the heavy object clasped in his arms.

"Oh, sir! I'm so glad you've come, sir!" Venables began as he skidded to a halt. "We've found the car, sir. It's only just round the corner."

"Thank goodness for that," Mr Wilkins replied thankfully. Now at least one of his problems was settled! He glanced from Venables to Darbishire, lumbering up to join the group, and asked, "Well, if you've found the car, why haven't you returned the jack?"

Darbishire bit his lip and looked down at the toes of his shoes. Coyly, he said, "We – er – we hoped you'd come with us and explain, sir. You see, it only drove up a couple of minutes ago, and then it stopped because – because . . ."

"Well, go on, boy. What did it stop for?"

"Because it had a flat tyre, sir. The driver's searching through his tool-kit for the jack. I – I think he wants to change the wheel, sir."

An explosive hiss burst from the master's lips as though he were attempting to imitate the sound of the motorist's punctured tyre; though in point of fact he was merely relieving his feelings.

Hurriedly, Venables broke in. "We thought it would sound better coming from you, sir. If *we* told him, he might think we'd taken it on purpose, but he'd be bound to listen to a master, wouldn't he, sir?"

Jennings nodded in agreement. "He'll probably be grateful to you for coming along in the nick of time, sir," he pointed out. "After all, he'd be in an awful mess without the jack, wouldn't he sir?"

Mr Wilkins was not impressed by this argument. The situation was completely out of hand. It really was too bad! The silly little boys couldn't be trusted to do the simplest thing without causing chaos and confusion. And as if that wasn't enough, they calmly expected him to put matters right!

With a grunt of annoyance he seized the jack from Darbishire and demanded to be told where the car had come to rest. Then, with the boys at his heels, he marched along the road and round the corner into the adjoining street.

Sure enough, an ancient green car, with a dented wing was parked by the kerbside. A thin, elderly man was rummaging through the boot. A flat tyre, on the rear nearside wheel, left no doubt as to what he was looking for.

For a moment Mr Wilkins paused, deciding what he would say by way of apology. He would have to choose his words with care, for naturally the man would be angry when he heard that the vital piece of equipment had been removed without permission.

"Is there anything we can do to help, sir?" asked Darbishire, noticing the master's hesitation.

"No, there certainly isn't!" retorted Mr Wilkins. "Things are bad enough without you boys making them worse!" He squared his shoulders and strode resolutely towards the car, determined at all costs to brave the fury of the motorist and explain the situation in a few well-chosen words.

The elderly motorist was so engrossed in his search that he was unaware of Mr Wilkins' approach. A series of polite, throat-clearing noises failed to attract his attention, so, with some diffidence, the master tapped him on the shoulder and said: "Er . . . Excuse me . . . I beg your pardon . . . Good afternoon!"

The motorist glanced up in startled surprise. He was a small, rather frail man, with a mild expression and a faraway look in his pale blue eyes. A thin, beaky nose, and the vague fluttering movements which he made with his hands, gave him an almost birdlike appearance. He had a fresh complexion and was clean-shaven apart from a few whispy tufts of white whisker about his cheeks suggesting that his mind had been occupied with other matters during his morning shave. After the first shock of surprise he peered at Mr Wilkins like a man trying to identify a face from the past.

"Oh . . . ah . . . Good afternoon, Mr Er – um," he mumbled gently. "Let me see, now. Have we met before? I don't seem to remember."

"No, we haven't met. My name's Wilkins and I want to apologise . . ."

"Oh, please don't apologise. I'm only too delighted to meet you, Mr Er – um – Mr Watkins," the old man twittered. "My name is Carr. You must forgive my not shaking hands, but they're not fit to be seen. My back wheel, you know."

"Yes, I had noticed you had a flat tyre," said Mr Wilkins sympathetically.

"Well, it's only flat at the bottom, of course, but I'm afraid it will have to be changed all the same." Mr Carr flapped his grimy fingers in the direction of the boot. "I don't quite know what to do. I've been searching through my tool box for the necessary implements, but I seem to have left the most important one at home."

This was Mr Wilkins' cue. He held up the missing tool and then set it down in the roadway with a thud. "Here you are. This is what you're looking for, I believe."

An expression of amazement passed across Mr Carr's birdlike features. He could not have looked more surprised if Mr Wilkins had produced a rabbit from a top hat.

"Why, so it is!" he exclaimed. "Well, well! Bless my soul! What an astonishing coincidence! And to think that you should happen to come along at the critical moment with the very tool I required! Would you allow me to borrow it for a few minutes? I'll be extremely careful."

It was clear that Mr Carr did not recognise his own

property, so Mr Wilkins did his best to put matters right.

"You don't have to borrow it – it's yours!" he explained.

"Oh, but I couldn't possibly accept it as a gift."

"I mean it belongs to you."

"Oh no, I think you're making a mistake. I just told you I find I've unfortunately left mine at home."

Mr Wilkins took a deep breath. He must be patient with the slow, wool-gathering wits of this charming old gentleman who persisted in misunderstanding everything that was said to him. In slow, deliberate tones, as though explaining some point of English grammar to the lowest form in the school, he said, "This – is – your – car – jack."

The elderly motorist nodded in agreement. "Of course it's my car; I've had it for years," he said. "But how did you know my name was Jack?"

"I didn't! I merely said . . ."

"Oh, but you did! You called me by my Christian name. I heard you."

Gently Mr Wilkins explained, "I only knew your name was Carr."

"Yes, that's right – Jack Carr."

It *would* be, Mr Wilkins reflected bitterly! Really this conversation was becoming impossible. He could not afford to waste the entire afternoon talking at cross purposes to this slow-witted old gentleman. With what patience he could muster he listened politely as J. Carr, Esq, rambled further and further away from the point.

". . . and you said to me, 'This is your car, Jack'. I distinctly heard you. Of course, it's just possible that you might have . . ."

Suddenly the words ceased and a look of understanding slowly spread over the birdlike features. Light was beginning to dawn. "Oh, wait a minute, though. Yes, of course! I see what you mean. You didn't mean 'this is your *car*, Jack, old boy,' – you meant 'This is your *jack*, Carr, old man'! Eh? H'm?"

"Er – yes; er – no, or rather . . ."

A ripple of chuckles showed that Mr Carr was savouring the joke to the full. "That's very good. Very amusing indeed! I must remember that. Jack Carr's car jack. You know, it's a funny thing but I never thought of it for myself. It reminds me of a similar sort of misunderstanding that happened to me many years ago when I was staying in the West Country . . ."

Anxious to stem the flow of reminiscence, Mr Wilkins said hurriedly, "Yes, well, anyway, here's the tool you're looking for, so you can go ahead if you want to change your wheel."

"Oh, thank you, Mr Er – um . . . It is most kind of you to take all this trouble to – er – to . . ."

Again the words faltered as Mr Carr peered at the jack in growing wonder. For now he looked more closely he felt sure he had seen it before somewhere. His eyesight and his memory were not what they used to be, of course, yet surely there was something familiar about the scratches around the base of the implement. After some seconds of close scrutiny light dawned again. Why, of course!

In the tones of one who has just made a sensational discovery he exclaimed, "Good gracious! Bless my soul! This *is* my jack, after all, you know!"

Mr Wilkins sighed. "That's what I've been trying to tell you for the last ten minutes."

"Yes, there's no doubt about it. I distinctly recognise it now I look more closely. Well, well! So I didn't leave it at home; it must have been in my tool-box all the time. Thank you so much for finding it for me, Mr Er – um – Mr Williams."

There was nothing to be gained by embarking on a further explanation, Mr Wilkins decided. If this well-meaning old gentleman was so slow in the uptake that it took him ten minutes to recognise his own property, it would take him a week to understand the series of events leading up to its disappearance. In that case it would be better to let sleeping dogs lie and not attempt any more apologies.

Briskly Mr Wilkins said, "That's all right, then. And if there's nothing more I can do I'll be getting along." He turned on his heel and was about to move away when the vague tones of Mr Carr again broke on his ear.

"Of course, Mr Er – um, there *is* one other thing, since you so kindly offered to help me."

Mr Wilkins swung round and forced a smile. "Yes, of course. Delighted. What can I do for you?"

"I wonder if you would be good enough to change the wheel for me? Of course, I hardly like to ask as it's a somewhat irksome task with this particular car. One has to crawl underneath and lie flat on one's back in order to get the jack in the one place where it can be relied upon to grip without slipping."

"Oh, no!" Mr Wilkins groaned beneath his breath. This was too much. This was the last straw! He would have something to say to those silly little boys when he got back to school.

"Unfortunately the rear axle oil leaks over the very spot where one is obliged to operate," Mr Carr explained in an apologetic twitter. "I usually keep an old mackintosh to wrap round my head, but I seem to have left it at home, unless, of course, you . . ." He focused his gaze upon Mr Wilkins' raincoat, and his eyes lit up as the solution dawned slowly in his mind. "Oh, but you *have* a mackintosh! How splendid!"

"I – I – Well, I mean to say, dash it all . . ."

"You're sure you don't mind, Mr Er – um? It's extremely kind of you to offer. Now, if you'd like to squeeze under the rear number plate I'll watch your feet for you."

"You'll do *what*?"

"Just in case any cars happen to pass too closely."

A shudder of horrified dismay ran through Mr Wilkins' frame. The prospect of ruining his raincoat and wounding his dignity was not one which he would normally have accepted without protest. And yet, what else could he do? For he was undoubtedly under an obligation to this old gentleman for the liberties that had been taken with his tools. Muttering, he knelt down and squirmed his way under the car in search of the one and only place where the jack could be relied upon to take a hold.

Mr Carr did his best to be helpful. He said "Tut-tut!" when Mr Wilkins bumped his head on the rear number plate. He deplored the leak from the back axle, and hoped that Mr Wilkins was not inconvenienced by the globules of oil dripping down on to his collar and trickling up his sleeves.

It is doubtful whether the unwilling mechanic heard the apologies or the words of encouragement. Lying cramped and uncomfortable below the creaking springs, his right eye closed against a cascade of oil from the rear axle, he was in no frame of mind to appreciate the well-meaning prattle of Jack Carr, Esq.

A high-pitched hum of conversation arose from the group of boys milling round the bus stop in the centre of Dunhambury High Street. Mr Carter glanced at his watch and frowned. Twenty-five to five! The bus was due to leave in a few minutes and as yet the party was not complete. His own group of boys was there and had, indeed, been waiting patiently for nearly a quarter of an hour. Shortly afterwards, an advance guard of Mr Wilkins' contingent, headed by Bromwich, had arrived, but so far there was no sign of the master in charge and the remaining members of his party. Mr Carter frowned again. What on earth was his colleague thinking of, to cut things so fine?

At that moment the three missing boys loomed into sight. Mr Carter beckoned to them and they broke into a trot, their cameras bumping up and down at the end of their straps.

"You boys are very late," the master observed, as Jennings and Venables slowed to a halt beside him. Darbishire, panting hard, was still some twenty yards down the road.

"Sorry, sir. We sort of got delayed," Jennings explained. "We're all here now, though, sir – even Darbishire's just about made it."

"But where's Mr Wilkins?"

"Oh, he's coming. He'll be here in a minute, sir. He told us to go on ahead."

Mr Carter nodded. With luck his colleague might yet be in time to catch the bus. Obviously, he must have spent longer than he had anticipated in pointing out the historic buildings and places of interest to the boys in his party.

"That's all right, then," Mr Carter remarked. "And were you boys able to take some good snapshots this afternoon?"

"Oh, yes, really good, sir," Jennings agreed enthusiastically.

"I thought you'd find plenty of suitable subjects in an old town like this."

"Yes, sir. I got a really good photo of the Dunhambury Fire Engine, sir!"

"Really!"

"And I got an even better one of the back of Jennings' head through the park railings, sir," Venables added. "Of course, when it comes out it'll probably look more like the back view of a car with both doors wide open, but that'll only be his ears, sir."

Mr Carter was mildly puzzled. It seemed an odd sort of subject for Mr Wilkins to suggest. He turned to the third latecomer and asked, "And did you take any photographs, Darbishire?"

"Yes, definitely, sir." Darbishire's eyes gleamed behind his dust-covered spectacles. "I took quite a lot, actually, but the best one was a real live action photo of Mr Wilkins underneath a car."

"Underneath a car!" Mr Carter echoed in alarm. "Good heavens! You don't mean there's been an accident?"

"Oh no, he's perfectly all right, sir. He went under of his own accord – more or less."

"Whatever has been going on?" the master demanded. "I thought he was going to stroll round with you offering advice on the way to . . ."

"Sir, please, sir! Here's Mr Wilkins coming now, sir."

The interruption came from Bromwich who was staring with a mixture of horror and delight at a tall figure tottering weakly towards the bus stop.

By now every head had swivelled round and every eye was following the direction of Bromwich's pointing finger. Eyebrows shot up in surprise and mouths which had opened to make apt comments remained agape in sheer astonishment . . . For the dazed and sorry-looking figure approaching them seemed a mere shadow of the brisk and bustling Mr Wilkins whom they knew so well.

He looked like a man reeling under some blow of fate. His hair was tousled, his face was grimy, his collar had broken loose from its top button and his tie was knotted beneath his left ear in a fashion often affected by Binns and Blotwell at breakfast time. Furthermore, the master's raincoat was streaked from shoulder to hem with oil and grease.

From the wild and staring look in his eyes it was obvious that he had recently passed through a harrowing experience. With trance-like steps he made his way along to the bus stop where he stood breathing heavily and glowering at the boys about him with marked disapproval.

"Good heavens, Wilkins, what on earth have you been doing?" Mr Carter exclaimed. "You're smothered in oil from head to foot, to say nothing of losing three buttons off your raincoat!"

"I know, Carter, I know. You don't have to tell me," his colleague muttered in a faint voice. "I've had a very trying afternoon, I don't mind telling you."

"I'm sorry to hear that. Didn't things go as we'd arranged?"

The bus drew up beside them at that moment and Mr Carter motioned to the boys to climb aboard. As they clattered past him, he continued, "But you told me you were merely going to stroll round the town with your party, helping them to take photographs of historic buildings. Surely nothing could go wrong with a simple plan like that!"

A flicker of anguish passed across his colleague's face. "Don't you believe it, Carter. With that silly little boy,

Jennings, in the party almost anything *could* happen – and practically everything *did*!"

He flung his arms skyward in a dramatic gesture that caused a passing pedestrian to leap aside in alarm. Wildly he declaimed, "Heads stuck in railings! . . . Fire-engines with no one to rescue! . . . Disappearing motorists with flat tyres and leaky gear-boxes! . . ."

"I don't understand," Mr Carter said as he stepped on to the platform of the bus and began to mount the stairs. "After all, we went out of our way to organise this outing properly."

"Maybe we did," grumbled Mr Wilkins, thumping heavily up the stairs behind his colleague. "And all I can say, Carter, is this: the next time we go out of our way to organise an outing, *you* can do the organising while *I* keep out of the way. I tell you I've had enough of it. False alarms! . . . Emergency calls! . . . Jack Carr and his car jack! . . ."

At that moment the conductor rang the bell and Mr Wilkins' further comments were mercifully drowned by the roar of the engine as the bus accelerated and sped on its way.

Chapter 9

Assorted Pets

All the way back to Linbury, the top deck of the bus hummed with the lively chatter of the returning photographers. With one notable exception, the whole party had enjoyed themselves and were determined that everybody else should hear about it. Details of the *Darbishire Method of Removing Heads from Railings* were described to those who had not been fortunate enough to see the demonstration, and the inventor was advised to take out a patent for his system. Temple entertained his fellow-travellers with a lecture on the latest fire-fighting appliances, and Venables explained how he, personally, would change a car wheel without crawling underneath the vehicle and getting his hands dirty.

Mr Carter sat back and listened with half an ear to the prattle and buzz going on around him. Once or twice he addressed a remark to his colleague, but he soon gave it up. Mr Wilkins, it seemed, was in no mood for small talk.

The misadventures of the afternoon had, for the time being, driven all thoughts of other matters from Jennings' mind. But when he arrived back at school and had eaten a hearty tea of baked beans on toast, he began once again to ponder over the whereabouts of his secret pet.

"It must be somewhere. It can't just have vanished into thin air, Darbi," he confided to his friend after tea that evening. "And nobody else can have found him or we should have heard about it by now."

A puzzled frown gathered on Darbishire's brow. "How's he managing for food, I'd like to know? It's some days since he beetled off without saying goodbye, so if he's still around these parts he must be getting a bit peckish by now."

Darbishire's concern was natural. After all, he was not to know that F. J. Saunders was at that moment gnawing his way though a carrot in Mr Wilkins' study. Even though he was not by nature a pet-lover, the master was attending to his duties in a kindly and efficient manner. He had grown accustomed to his role of animal-keeper now that the guinea-pig had been in his charge for the best part of a week. At times he would even let it out for a run round the hearthrug, but he always took good care to see that the door of his room was shut before he opened the box.

Thus there was no real cause to worry about the guinea-pig's welfare. Had Jennings and Darbishire known that it was in safe hands all might have been well . . . The trouble was that they didn't know, and had no means of finding out.

"Look at it this way, Darbi. Put yourself in F. J. Saunders' place," Jennings reasoned as the dormitory bell sounded and they went upstairs to bed. "Supposing you got lost and were wandering about in search of board and lodging, where would you go?"

Darbishire wrinkled his nose in thought. "I'd make for the tuck cupboard," he decided. "There'd be masses to eat there – liquorice allsorts, marshmallows, butterscotch, and a whole lot of that homemade fudge that Martin-Jones's mother sent him last week."

Jennings clicked his teeth in exasperation. "Don't be

such a shrimp-witted clodpoll, Darbi. Guinea-pigs don't eat marshmallows and homemade fudge!"

"I never said they did!" Darbishire defended himself. "You asked me where *I'd* go, and I said . . ."

"All right, all right! But suppose you *were* a guinea-pig. You'd want things like brussels sprouts and carrots and stuff, wouldn't you?"

Darbishire conceded the point. "In that case I'd probably go snooping round the dustbins, or make a beeline for the kitchen garden."

"Exactly," Jennings agreed. "You wouldn't stay indoors at all. And that's where we've made our big mistake. We've been looking in the wrong places. I bet you what you like, F. J. Saunders has found himself a hideout in the potting shed, nice and handy for the spring greens and things in the vegetable plot."

It was too late and too dark to start a new line of investigation that evening, but as they prepared for bed Jennings sketched out new plans for a thorough search of the kitchen garden the following day.

The middle of the afternoon would be the best time to carry out the operation, he decided. There would be half an hour to spare between the end of football and the beginning of afternoon school. That should be long enough for them to make their way along the rows of spring vegetables, scrutinising every leaf for some sign of the missing pet. Moreover, it was unlikely that their movements would be observed by anyone in authority, for at that hour of the afternoon the masters would be refreshing themselves with cups of tea for the labours that awaited them in the classrooms.

"That's what we'll do, then," Jennings whispered to Darbishire as Mr Carter came in to put out the dormitory light. "Hurry up and get changed as fast as you can after football, and then we'll beetle off on our hunting expedition while the coast's still clear."

The search for Saunders turned out to be a more hazardous task than the organiser of the expedition had supposed. As soon as the final whistle blew the following afternoon, Jennings and Darbishire scampered off the football field at the double and reached the changing-room well ahead of the rest of the players.

It took them four minutes to change back into their day clothes, and a further thirty seconds to assure themselves that all the masters were either drinking tea in the dining-hall, or were chivvying the slower changers out of the shower-bath room with cries of encouragement and threats of detention.

The coast was clear. They hurried out of the building and in through the gate of the kitchen garden. Then, after a fruitless search of the potting shed, they made their way on hands and knees along the rows of vegetables, examining each plant for some sign of the missing pet. It was slow, backbreaking work, and after a while Darbishire began to feel that their quest was in vain.

"This is hopeless, Jen," he complained, wiping his soil-smeared hands on his sweater. "I've searched these beetroots leaf by leaf, and there isn't a whisker of him anywhere. I vote we go back and have another look in the potting shed."

"Ssh! Ssh!"

Was it his fancy, Jennings wondered, or had his ear caught a rustling sound amongst the turnip tops a little way over to his left? With his fingers to his lips he repeated the order for silence. "Ssh, Darbi! Ssh!"

"What did you say?" Darbishire demanded loudly, looking up from his beetroot.

"I said 'Ssh'! I thought I heard something."

"Yes, so did I."

"You did! Goodo!" If they had both heard the sound it could not have been his imagination. "What did it sound like to you?"

"It was a sort of hissing noise."

Jennings *tut-tutted* in reproach. "Don't be such a crazy clodpoll, Darbi. That was me saying 'Ssh'!"

"Oh, sorry."

"Didn't you hear a sort of swooshing scritch-scratch sort of sound coming out of the turnips? Listen!"

They knelt in silence, holding their breath and straining their ears for the telltale sound. After ten seconds Darbishire gave up the unequal struggle and let out his pent-up breath with a noise like an electric train applying its vacuum brakes.

"*Pheeew!* Sorry, Jen, I just couldn't hold it in any longer!"

The miniature explosion with which Darbishire had shattered the stillness of the afternoon had an unexpected result. There was a sudden fluttering of the turnip tops away to their left as though some animal had taken fright.

"There he is!" Jennings croaked in a voiceless whisper. "Look at those leaves shaking. There's something under them, right enough!"

Moving with extreme care they rose to their feet and tiptoed across the spring greens, stepping high over the plants until they reached the turnip patch. Stealth and caution were essential. The hunted animal must not suspect that the net was closing in.

The leaves had stopped rustling by now, but the animal's

former movements had betrayed its position. Jennings crouched down and beckoned to Darbishire to take up a position on the opposite edge of the turnip plot, ready to block the way of escape in his direction. Then, with a slow and stealthy movement, he edged back the leaves over the spot where he knew their quarry must be.

As he did so, he caught sight of a moving bundle of fur. He made a quick, deft grab, hoisted the animal clear of the surrounding foliage – and found himself holding a medium-sized ginger-coloured cat in his arms.

"Oh, fish-hooks!" he exclaimed in dismay. "It's only George the Third after all!"

There was no doubt about the identity of the cat. Matron's ginger tom, George the Third, was a well-known member of the Linbury community and was frequently to be observed sunning himself on a classroom window ledge, or hurrying across the playground on some mysterious errand of his own. He was a dignified animal, devoted to his mistress, but distrustful of boys who tried to make a fuss of him. His high-sounding title was not due to royal ancestry, but to the fact that he was the third generation of a feline family which Matron had adopted some years earlier.

Jennings shook his head in self-reproach. "Tut! I ought to have guessed, I suppose. Matron says he often comes into the kitchen garden in the afternoon."

A sudden look of alarm passed over Darbishire's features as his friend replaced the cat gently but firmly amongst the turnip tops.

"I say, Jen! Do you think its safe to let him go wandering around like that? Supposing F. J. Saunders is somewhere in the garden after all. Supposing they met face to face! Cats and guinea-pigs don't mix, you know."

Darbishire had certainly raised a point. There was every reason to keep a watchful eye on George the Third until they knew for certain whether or not the guinea-pig was still within the school precincts.

"Pick him up then, Darbi," Jennings decided. "You'll have to carry him while I get on with the search."

Somewhat to their surprise Matron's cat responded well to Darbishire's overtures of friendship.

"Good puss. Come to Uncle," he said as he lifted the animal into his arms. "Hey, Jen, he likes me! He's purring like a jumbo jet!"

"Just as well. You may have to look after him for some time yet."

The worried look returned to Darbishire's eyes. "But I can't, Jen. What happens when the bell goes for afternoon school? I can't go waltzing into Old Wilkie's lesson with my arms full of George the Third!"

"We'll have to press on with the hunt really quickly, that's all then," was Jennings' comment. His glance swept over the foliage at his feet and followed the rows of cabbages to the gate at the far end of the garden. Suddenly his expression changed.

"Crystallized cheesecakes!" he exlaimed.

"What's up? Seen something?" asked Darbishire, straining his eyes in the wrong direction.

Jennings nodded grimly.

"F. J. Saunders?" came the hopeful query.

"No, L. P. Wilkins. He's just coming through the gate and he's got us in his gunsights. I should say he's getting up steam for a roof-level attack, from the look of him."

Mr Wilkins' attention had first been drawn to the fact that something unusual was afoot when, having finished his cup of tea in the dining-hall, he had made his way upstairs to his study. A message from Mr Pemberton-Oakes had informed him that Atkinson's grandmother would be calling during the afternoon to take away the guinea-pig which, mindless of school rules, she had left in his charge.

Mr Wilkins was almost sorry to hear that his stock-rearing duties were coming to an end. He had grown quite fond of the little animal. The least he could do was to make sure that it was well supplied with food for the return journey. With this in mind he entered his study and removed the lid of the box which did duty as a cage . . . All was in order. There was enough fodder left to keep the hungriest of guinea-pigs happy for the rest of the day.

It was then that Mr Wilkins glanced out of the window. A puzzled frown creased his brow, for his first-floor room commanded a clear view over the hedge and into the kitchen garden beyond . . . And there, crawling along the rows of cabbages on their hands and knees, were two figures who had no business to be in the garden at all.

This was a matter that called for immediate investigation, he decided. By taking prompt action he would catch them redhanded.

He shot out of the room like a fighter pilot in an ejector seat, slamming the door behind him with a thud. But in his haste to catch the furtive crawlers he completely forgot to replace the lid on the guinea-pig's box.

F. J. Saunders was a rodent with a taste for roaming. Very soon a pink snout and a set of bristling whiskers rose above the rim of the box. A pair of beady eyes surveyed the surroundings with curious interest; and a moment later a white furry body struggled out of the makeshift cage and set off on a tour of the hearthrug.

*   *   *   *

94

Jennings' fears about Mr Wilkins' frame of mind were more than justified.

"What are you boys doing in the kitchen garden?" the master demanded angrily as he marched through the gate and stamped his way up towards the small-game hunters. "You know perfectly well you're out of bounds. You haven't had permission to come in here, have you?"

"No, sir."

"Then I fail to understand . . ." The angry tone faltered for a moment and a note of bewilderment crept into the master's voice as he demanded, "And what, in the name of thunder, are you nursing that cat for, Darbishire?"

Darbishire gave a nervous laugh. "Nothing, sir. That is, nothing much, as you might say. I – er – I found him in the turnips, sir, and I picked him up because – well, we didn't really think it was safe to let him go wandering about all over the place."

"Not safe! What are you talking about, boy! I don't know what ridiculous game you boys are playing, but whatever it is I'm not going to have it!" Mr Wilkins went on in rising anger, "Go up to my room and wait for me there! I've had just about enough of you and your senseless pranks, and I'm going to get to the bottom of this business, or know the reason why!"

"Yes, sir."

There were still a few minutes left before the bell was due for afternoon school when the two boys reached the door of Mr Wilkins' study. Darbishire still held Matron's cat in his arms. He had been afraid to put it down in the garden in case the guinea-pig should, after all, be lurking amongst the vegetation; and by the time he had hurried indoors he was scarcely aware of the animal's presence. Outside Mr Wilkins' door he came out of his absent-minded trance and put the cat down gently on the floor.

"Old Wilkie did say we must wait *inside* his room, didn't he?" he asked nervously. "Or do you think he meant us to wait outside in the corridor?"

Jennings hunched his shoulders and pulled a long face. "I don't know. There's sure to be a hoo-hah whichever we do, as soon as he hears about F. J. Saunders." He opened the door and advanced into the room. "The trouble is, of course, that he'll simply refuse to believe us when we tell him we've found a guinea-pig actually on the premises."

"We haven't *found* one – we've lost one!" Darbishire pointed out. "And that makes it more difficult in a way. How can we prove there ever was a . . ."

"Wow!"

Jennings' sudden shout of surprise cut across the gloomy forebodings. In two bounds he had crossed the room and stooped to pick up a small furry bundle from the hearthrug.

"Here he is, look! F. J. Saunders, himself, in person! As large as life!"

Darbishire's eyes were round as saucers as he stared at the missing pet. "I can't believe it," he gasped. "How did he get here? What's he doing here? Who let him in?"

"I don't know!" Jennings retorted impatiently. "Perhaps he got on the track of that raw cabbage Old Wilkie's so fond of, and decided to pop in for a quick snack while no one was about."

"Just as well Old Wilkie *isn't* about," Darbishire agreed. "He'd get in a frantic bate if he knew there was a guinea-pig at large in his study. We'd better get Saunders out of here pretty quickly before he comes up and finds him."

There was no time to argue the question of how or why the secret pet had reappeared in so surprising a fashion. Mr

Wilkins was known to be on his way up to the study; if the guinea-pig was to be saved from his clutches something must be done without delay!

As they debated their best course of action they were made aware of an even more urgent need to remove F. J. Saunders to a place of safety . . . For in through the open door stalked George the Third, tail erect and whiskers a-quiver.

With a cry of horror, Darbishire stooped and gathered the cat once more into his arms. Mr Wilkins might express himself tersely on the subject of guinea-pigs, but Matron's cat was a foe with whom it was not even possible to argue.

For some seconds the boys stood on either side of the room clutching their respective animals. Then Jennings said, "We'll have to shut the cat up in here, and take Saunders outside till we've found something to put him in. If only we'd got a cage, or something . . ."

"I know where there is one," Darbishire interrupted.

"You do? Goodo! Where?"

"Upstairs in the attic. Mr Carter told me to take some old books up there one day last week, and I saw it in the corner along with a lot of ancient bedsteads and that sort of junk."

Jennings looked doubtful. "What sort of a cage is it?"

"Well, it's a bird cage, really," Darbishire explained apologetically. "But it'd do to be going on with, wouldn't it? It's quite a good size. I reckon someone on the staff must have kept a parrot or something way back in Julius Caesar's time."

A parrot cage, though not designed for the purpose, would at least offer a temporary solution to the housing problem. So, leaving Matron's cat purring contentedly in Mr Wilkins' armchair, Jennings and Darbishire with their newly-found pet, hastened from the room and closed the door behind them.

There was still no sign of Mr Wilkins as they tiptoed along the corridor and climbed the flight of narrow stairs leading to the top floor.

The un-oiled hinges of the attic door creaked in protest as Jennings turned the knob and led the way into the room. The light was dim, for stacked in front of the only window was an array of broken furniture and the remains of scenery from school plays acted long ago. Dusty books and faded school photographs lay in heaps upon the floor, and an old-fashioned magic lantern was balanced precariously on top of a tall mahogany bookcase.

"There you are, you see. Just the job, eh?"

With a triumphant gesture Darbishire pointed to a parrot cage suspended from a nail in the wall. It was some inches out of his reach, so he looked round for something to stand on and finally selected a rusty iron bedstead which he trundled across the floor to the opposite wall.

The bumps and thuds resulting from this operation caused Jennings to grimace in alarm. "Ssh! Quiet, Darbi! Don't make such a row! If anyone hears us up here they'll want to know what's going on."

For safety's sake he closed and latched the door, although the creaking of the hinges made nearly as much noise as Darbishire's efforts to move the bedstead.

"You'd better climb up and get it. I've got my hands full of F. J. Saunders," Jennings said. Faintly from below he could hear the bell sounding for afternoon school. "And you'd better hurry up about it. We've got to report back to Old Wilkie before we go into class."

"Righto. You be ready to hold the old bed steady in case it collapses."

"You mean hold the bedstead. There's no such thing as a bed-steady."

"I mean be ready to hold the bedstead steady, instead of wasting time arguing about what I mean!" Darbishire retorted curtly. Then he climbed up on the iron framework and lifted down the parrot cage.

From his elevated perch he found he could see out of the window. Down below on the playground, boys were hurrying indoors in response to the summons of the bell. He was about to jump down off the bed when he caught sight of a car which had drawn up on the playground. Beside it stood Mr Wilkins in conversation with a middle-aged woman who had obviously just emerged from the driving seat.

Darbishire frowned thoughtfully. This would explain why the master had not yet followed them up to his room. The delay, however, was only temporary, for even as he watched, the visitor made off towards the main entrance, while Mr Wilkins turned and hurried in through the side door leading up to his study.

Darbishire caught his breath in sudden alarm. There was not a moment to lose if they were to be outside his room waiting for him when he arrived.

"Quick, Jen, quick!" he urged. "Old Wilkie's just coming in!"

"I can't be quick! I've got Saunders to look after," Jennings protested as he picked up the rusty wire cage. "You nip down to Old Wilkie's room and keep him talking till I get there."

"What shall I say? I can't talk about the weather. And he's sure to ask where you are."

"Tell him I've been detained. Say I'm just coming."

"Yes, but . . ."

"Oh, for goodness' sake get a move on, Darbi. He'll be there in two bats of an eyelid!"

With feverish haste Jennings seized the handle, intending to fling wide the door for Darbishire's speedy exit. As he pulled, the knob came away in his hand, while from the passage outside came a little thud as the other end of the knob, with the spindle attached, dropped down on to the floor.

"Oh, fish-hooks!" he cried in despair as he stared at the useless doorknob in his hand.

"Now what's happened?" Darbishire demanded nervously.

"It's this wretched handle. It's come out."

"Well, bung it back again, quick! Old Wilkie will be halfway up the stairs by now."

"I can't put it back – that's the trouble! The screw came out when I pulled it and the other end with the bar on is rolling about the passage."

Darbishire sprang to the door and then recoiled in horror and dismay as the truth burst upon him.

"You mean we're trapped!"

Jennings nodded. "And it's no good shaking or pushing it. The latch won't turn unless the handle's in, and as we've lost the part that matters, it means this door can only be opened from the other side!"

Chapter 10

The Last of F. J. Saunders

As the bell for afternoon school ceased ringing, Mr Carter emerged from the dining-hall and strolled slowly towards the staff-room. He had no class to take for the first lesson and he intended to use his free time in marking English essays.

Unfortunately, his good intentions came to nothing, for as he reached the foot of the stairs the door leading to the playground hurtled open as though a small charge of dynamite had been placed behind it. Over the threshold came Mr Wilkins, hurrying with the set purpose of one who has urgent business to attend to.

"I say, Carter, I wonder if you'd do me a favour?" he boomed as he strode up to his colleague. "I shall be a few minutes late in getting into class for the first lesson. Would you mind keeping an eye on my form till they've settled down?"

"Certainly," Mr Carter agreed. "I've a free period as it happens. Do you want me to set them some work, or have they got something to be going on with?"

"Well, if you wouldn't mind coming up to my room with me, I'll let you have their history books to give back. I've just marked their last prep, so they can read it through and do their corrections while they're waiting. You needn't stay with them."

On the way upstairs Mr Wilkins explained the reasons

for this minor alteration in the timetable.

"Atkinson's grandmother has just arrived to take that guinea-pig away," he said. "She's gone up to the sick-room to see how the boy's getting on, and I promised I'd take it along to her before I went into class."

The passage outside Mr Wilkins' room was empty, but this fact did not worry him unduly. Presumably Jennings and Darbishire had gone off to their classroom when the bell rang. In any case, there would be time enough to deal with them later on, when the more pressing business of Mrs Atkinson's livestock had been settled.

The first thing that caught Mr Wilkins' eye when he opened his study door was that the guinea-pig's box was empty; whereas the armchair was full – occupied by a medium-sized ginger cat washing its whiskers and looking very pleased with itself.

Panic and alarm seized Mr Wilkins.

"Good heavens! I – I! What's happened?" he burst out. "Where's that wretched rodent? How did that cat get there? What's been going on?"

Mr Carter made no attempt to answer the string of questions. It seemed to him that his colleague was leaping to hasty conclusions. Surely a medium-sized cat would not attack so large an animal as a guinea-pig? . . . Or would it? He could not be sure. There was no sign of a struggle; but then, there was no sign of the guinea-pig, either, although they searched the room from end to end. The whole thing was most mysterious.

"It looks as though you may have to tell Mrs Atkinson that she's seen the last of her pet," he observed at length. "You'll have to explain that owing to an unfortunate accident the guinea-pig got out . . ."

"Yes, yes, yes, but how did the cat get *in*?" interrupted

Mr Wilkins. "My study door was closed. I distinctly remember shutting it behind me when I went down to the kitchen garden to . . ." He paused as the obvious answer flashed into his mind. "Wait! I see what's happened. It was those stupid boys, Jennings and Darbishire! They were carrying the cat when I sent them up here!"

"You suggest that they shut it up in your room and calmly walked off?"

"What else could have happened?" demanded Mr Wilkins in exasperated tones. "They must be off their heads! Nobody in their senses would do a thing like that. It's all thanks to Jennings that this has happened. Just wait till I see that boy again!"

"Quite. But in the meantime Mrs Atkinson is waiting to see *you*," Mr Carter reminded him. "She may not be very pleased when she finds she's come all this way to retrieve a precious pet which Jennings and the cat between them have carelessly mislaid. She'll probably remind you that it was left in your charge."

"*Doh!* It's not my fault, Carter," Mr Wilkins defended himself. "The trouble I've taken over that animal's welfare! I couldn't have lavished more care and attention on it if I'd been grooming it for a prizewinner at a rodent show. And now, what am I going to say to Mrs Atkinson? Tell me that, Carter. What am I going to say?"

Mr Carter shook his head. "I don't know, Wilkins. I suggest you see what she's got to say first. And now, if you'll excuse me, I'll be getting along to keep an eye on your class."

Dejected in spirit, Mr Wilkins followed his colleague from the room and hurried off to the sick-room at the far end of the landing.

Meanwhile, upstairs in the attic, the situation was

growing more desperate every minute.

"We may be stuck here for hours – days, even," Jennings lamented, after all their efforts to open the door had ended in failure. "Nobody ever comes up here as a rule, and if we shout for help I don't suppose they'll hear us."

Darbishire was quick to spot the flaw in this argument. "Ah, but when we first came in, you told me to be quiet because everyone *would* hear us."

"That was when the door was open," Jennings pointed out curtly. "Besides, there's no one about now they've all gone into class."

"What shall we do, then?"

Thanks to Jennings, a solution to the problem was soon forthcoming. The attic in which they were imprisoned was situated immediately above the sick-room on the floor below. If they could attract the attention of the convalescent Atkinson and warn him of their plight, he might be persuaded to come upstairs and open the door from the outside.

"Or, if he's not allowed out of the sick-room, he could tell Matron, and she could do it instead," Jennings explained. "I wouldn't mind *her* knowing we were up here. She's OK. It's people like Old Wilkie we've got to steer clear of."

"Yes, but how do we get in touch with Atki if he can't hear us when we shout?"

"We don't need to shout. We'll tap on the window until he looks out to see what's going on. Then, we can call down and tell him."

The equipment needed for communication with the room below consisted of a makeshift window-knocker and a piece of string upon which it could be suspended. There was no shortage of materials in the attic, and Jennings lost no time in removing the string from a couple of brown paper parcels lying on a shelf and knotting together a sufficient length to reach the sick-room window. Before starting wor' he transferred the guinea-pig to his blazer pocket where immediately burrowed under his handkerchief and went sleep.

"We might as well use the parrot cage for a window-tapper," he decided. "It's not too heavy to let down, and Atki will be bound to hear it."

A few moments later they had edged round the wardrobe, opened the window, and were dangling the bird cage outside the sick-room window on the storey below. The window-tapper swung to and fro like a pendulum on the end of its string, and then bumped gently but audibly against the glass.

Operation Rescue was under way.

If Mr Wilkins had not been so agitated about the fate of the missing pet, his efforts to explain matters to Mrs Atkinson might have been more successful. As it was, his garbled apologies were so obscure that she had not the faintest idea what he was talking about when he burst into the sick-room where she was chatting to her grandson.

"Ah, there you are, Mrs Atkinson. I'm terribly sorry, but the most extraordinary thing has happened," Mr Wilkins began. "I can't explain because I don't understand how it occurred, but I assure you I shall take steps to see that those responsible are soundly punished and won't have a chance to do it again."

"I don't understand," she replied. "Who won't do what again?"

"The two boys I found in the vegetable garden! They had no right to shut George the Third in my study. Who'd have thought they'd have done anything so incredibly foolish!"

The reference to George the Third left Mrs Atkinson more perplexed than ever. What did the royal House of Hanover have to do with the subject under discussion?

"It's most unfortunate, of course, and I do apologise, but these things happen occasionally, even in the best regulated schools, you know."

"Please come to the point, Mr Wilkins. What is it you're trying to tell me?"

"Well, it's like this. I'm afraid you must be prepared for an unexpected shock."

The warning was apt. The unexpected shock occurred so suddenly that everyone in the room was startled into speechless surprise.

For even as Mr Wilkins finished his sentence there came a tapping upon the window. Wheeling round, they saw a large parrot cage swinging in space beyond the glass and bumping against the pane with a slow and steady rhythm. *Knock, knock, knock* . . . Pause . . . *Knock, knock, knock*.

Mr Wilkins was the first to recover the power of speech, though what he had to say shed little light upon the strange phenomenon.

"I – I – *Corwumph!*" he spluttered. "What – what – what? Who on earth . . . ! Goodness gracious! I've never, in all my life . . . What in the name of thunder is going on up there?"

Atkinson bounced up and down on his bed in high-spirited glee. "Oh, sir! Really exciting, isn't it, sir? What do you think it is, sir?"

"I don't know, but I'll soon find out!"

With a muttered apology the master rushed out of the sick-room like a rugger forward breaking loose from the scrum, leaving his visitor bemused with shock. She knew little about the routine of a boys' school. Yet even so, it seemed incredible to her that anyone in their senses should wish to spend the afternoon beating a tattoo upon an upstairs window with a parrot cage suspended on a piece of string. It was all very confusing!

A sound like a squad of infantry marking time in army boots announced that Mr Wilkins was pounding up the stairs to the top floor two at a time.

"Who is in this room?" he demanded angrily as he approached the attic door.

"Please, sir, it's us – Jennings and Darbishire, sir," came from within.

Jennings and Darbishire – *it would be*!

"Open the door at once!"

"We can't, sir. We're marooned. The knob's fallen out into the passage on your side, sir."

A downward glance proved this to be correct. With bad grace Mr Wilkins picked up the knob and inserted the spindle in the lock. Then he flung open the door and glared angrily at the two woebegone figures fidgeting from foot to foot in shamefaced embarrassment.

"What's going on here? What are you boys doing in the attic?"

"Trying to get out, sir."

"Yes, I know that, you silly little boy! But what did you go in for, in the first place?"

Jennings looked down at the toes of his shoes. "Well, you see, sir, you told us to report to you."

"You didn't expect to find me up here amongst the rubbish, did you?"

"Oh, no, sir. Only, Matron's cat was stalking about

downstairs, you see, and we didn't think it was safe, so we came up here to get the birdcage, sir."

Mr Wilkins' eyebrows shot up like window blinds. "You mean to tell me you were going to put Matron's cat in a birdcage?"

"Oh, no, sir," Jennings assured him. Really, Mr Wilkins was being very difficult. If he persisted in asking such awkward questions there would be nothing for it but to tell him the whole story.

Sorrowfully, he began, "Well, sir, you know there's a rule about not keeping pets . . ."

The words seemed to affect Mr Wilkins strangely. Pets! . . . Cats! . . . Guinea-pigs! . . . Grandmothers! . . . And silly little boys whose senseless meddling in other people's affairs had caused more trouble than they could ever realise. Would he ever get to the root of this extraordinary muddle?

He glanced down at Jennings stumbling through his long-winded explanation: and as he did so he noticed a curious thing . . . The boy's blazer pocket was bulging – and the bulge was moving! Could it be the answer to the mystery?

"Jennings. What *have* you got in your pocket?" Mr Wilkins demanded.

"Only this, sir," Jennings replied as he produced a wriggling, furry bundle for the master's inspection.

"The guinea-pig!" The words came in a shout. "But – but – what are you doing with it? How did it get in your pocket?"

"I just put it there for the time being. After we'd finished tapping on the window I was going to put my guinea-pig in the cage, sir."

"*Your* guinea-pig!" Mr Wilkins retorted sharply. "What

do you mean, *your* guinea-pig? It's *my* guinea-pig!"

Jennings' jaw dropped, and he opened his eyes wide in amazement. "Oh, but sir, it can't be yours, sir. I found it last week, only I lost it again."

"And I lost it last week and then I found it again. I've been looking after it for Atkinson's grandmother."

Jennings and Darbishire stared at him in puzzled wonder. Not knowing the full facts of the case, this fragment of information seemed almost impossible to believe.

Suddenly, a small part of the puzzle clicked into place like a jigsaw in Darbishire's brain.

"Oh, so that's what you wanted those cabbage leaves for, sir!" he exclaimed.

"Well, of course it was! You don't imagine I wanted to eat them myself, do you?"

"Well, we did rather wonder, sir."

"*Doh!* Of all the trumpery tomfoolery . . ."

But this was not the time for a detailed discussion as to how and why the misunderstanding had arisen. For the moment it was enough that the missing pet had reappeared in time to be given back to its rightful owner.

"Put that animal in the parrot cage, Jennings. It will do for Mrs Atkinson to take it home in," Mr Wilkins ordered. "And you can both report to me at the end of the lesson. It's time you were taught to behave in a responsible fashion!"

When the pair had scurried off to their classroom, Mr Wilkins returned to the sick-room carrying F. J. Saunders in the birdcage. Even though he could now explain matters to Mrs Atkinson, he was still feeling somewhat perturbed. Thanks to Jennings, he had had a very trying and nerve-racking quarter of an hour.

"Guinea-pigs! *Tut!* . . . Grandmothers! *Tut!* . . ." Mr Wilkins muttered beneath his breath as he walked along the corridor.

If he had *his* way, he told himself, he would not only ban pets from the school premises – he would ban grand-mothers as well!

By the time Mrs Atkinson had taken her leave, the first lesson of the afternoon was drawing to its close. Mr Wilkins reached his classroom to find that little more than five minutes remained in which to impart to Form Three a few facts about the reign of Edward the First.

He wasted no time. While still some ten yards from the open door of the classroom he boomed out his instructions to the earnest seekers after knowledge awaiting his arrival.

"Hurry up now, you boys. Open your history text books at Chapter Nine. Quickly, now, we've got a lot of work to get through."

Form Three *tut-tutted* in disappointment. Since Mr Carter had looked in to return their history books nearly half an hour before, no master had appeared to take charge of the form. Hopes had run high that the whole lesson might be spent in this blissful state of freedom. Apart from Jennings and Darbishire, who had arrived when the period was half over, the rest of the boys had enjoyed this unexpected change in the timetable.

Temple and Bromwich had spent the time playing indoor cricket. Thompson had rearranged his stamp collection. Venables and Rumbelow had enjoyed a delightful twenty minutes playing darts with Jennings' pen, until the nib had snapped off short and they had been obliged to seek some other form of amusement.

Now, it seemed, their brief respite was over, but they were still in holiday mood and slow to force their minds back to work. They shuffled in their seats and thumbed their way vaguely through the pages of their history books.

"Have you all got the place?" Mr Wilkins demanded, striding up to the master's desk. "Chapter Nine. Right then! We're going to start . . ."

"Please, sir, which chapter is it, sir?" asked Temple.

"Chapter Nine."

"Chapter *Nine*, sir?"

"You heard what I said!"

"I just wanted to make sure."

"Right! Well, this chapter tells us . . ."

Venables hand shot towards the ceiling. "Excuse me, sir. Which chapter did you say it was?"

Mr Wilkins glared at the offender. "Why don't you silly little boys listen? I've already told you the chapter four times!"

"Sorry, sir."

"Did you say Chapter *Four*, sir?" queried Bromwich, emerging from beneath his desk lid. "I thought you said Chapter Nine just now."

There was a loud bang as Mr Wilkins thumped the master's desk in exasperation.

"This class is the limit! I've just told you – Chapter Four for the ninth time – er – I mean, Chapter Nine for the fourth time."

"That's the fifth time," muttered Darbishire beneath his breath.

When at last everybody had found the place, Mr Wilkins began.

"Now, this chapter tells us about the reign of Edward the First, 1272–1307, who was the first king to hold a proper Parliament and introduce ideas of law and justice into the country."

At that point the bell rang for the end of the period. Form Three were delighted. The shorter the lesson the better, as far as they were concerned.

But Mr Wilkins was annoyed that so little had been accomplished. It was all the fault of those silly little boys for delaying him with that stupid nonsense in the attic! He glanced at the desks in the back row where the two culprits were nerving themselves for the ordeal they had to face.

Jennings raised his hand. "Please, sir, you said we were to report to you at the end of the lesson."

"I certainly did," snapped Mr Wilkins. "I've just about had enough of you and Darbishire. For the last week you've consistently caused an endless amount of trouble with your irresponsible behaviour and disobedience. Today, I find you breaking bounds in the vegetable garden and concealing the whereabouts of that wretched animal while I was searching high and low for it. You'll both be off games for a fortnight, and you can take a red stripe against your House in your conduct books."

All things considered, this seemed an inadequate punishment, and he sought in his mind for some way of increasing the severity of the sentence. His eye fell upon the history book open on the desk before him.

"And in addition, you will copy out in your best handwriting the first six pages of Chapter Nine in your history book. Start immediately after school and bring the work to me on Monday."

"Yes, sir," said Darbishire obediently, but Jennings raised his hand once more.

"Please, sir, I haven't got a pen," he pointed out. "I found it broken when I came into class."

Venables and Rumbelow assumed expressions of wide-eyed innocence. They hadn't *meant* to cause any damage: it was just one of those things that were liable to happen during a lively game of darts.

"So I can't start yet, sir. Not until I . . ."

"Silence, boy!" the master thundered. A wave of indignation swept over him and his complexion turned three shades pinker at the very idea of his orders being discussed in this manner. If the boy had imagined he could postpone or minimise his punishment by putting forward some ridiculous excuse, he would find that his foolhardiness would have exactly the opposite effect.

"Very well, Jennings. Since you have no pen you can *learn* the six pages instead!"

Jennings was appalled at the task that lay before him. "Oh, sir! Learn them by heart, sir! All of them, sir?"

"That's what I said. Word perfect. I'll give you until tomorrow week to learn it, and I'll hear you say it during the history lesson in the afternoon."

"But, sir! Six whole pages by tomorrow week, sir! It'll take me every minute of my spare time."

A satisfied smile hovered for a moment about the corners of Mr Wilkins' lips.

"That, my dear boy," he said in a fatherly tone, "is the whole point of the punishment."

Chapter 11

Contributions in Kind

It was the usual practice at Linbury Court for the staff to foregather in their common room during mid-morning break. Here they could relax over tea and biscuits, undisturbed by the shrill voices and clattering footwear of the seventy-nine boarders on the playground.

When Mr Carter entered the room the following morning he found most of his colleagues already assembled. The headmaster had not yet put in an appearance, but Matron was there, chatting with Mr Hind, a tall, thin man with a quiet voice who taught art and music. Mr Topliss (French and Latin) was discussing football with Mr Goddard (Geography and Woodwork), and various other members of the staff were reading the newspapers or frowning over *The Times* crossword puzzle.

Mr Wilkins sat back in an armchair, his cup of tea perched precariously upon the arm. On his lap was a pile of Form Four maths books which he had collected at the end of the previous lesson.

"Hullo, Wilkins," Mr Carter greeted him. "I hear you were successful, after all, in tracing Mrs Atkinson's guinea-pig yesterday afternoon."

Mr Wilkins nodded. "Yes, but I wasted a whole history lesson with Form Three in consequence," he said gloomily. "And if there's one class in the school which can't afford to waste time, it's Form Three. I tell you, frankly, they're turning my hair grey. There are more half-wits to the square metre in that class than in any other in the school."

His colleague smiled reproachfully at the exaggeration. "Surely, Wilkins, they're not as bad as all that?"

"If you ask me, Carter, they're a lot *worse* than all that!"

"I admit their work is nothing to write home about," Mr Carter conceded, as he poured himself a cup of tea. "The Head's rather concerned about it. He was saying the other day that he shuddered to think what would happen if an inspector were to put them through their paces."

"Exactly! Take that boy Jennings, for instance. He's easily the most . . ." The words ceased abruptly and Mr Wilkins sat up straight in his chair as the significance of his colleague's remark dawned upon him. Anxiously he asked, "What was that you said then?"

"I said Form Three weren't as bad as you make out."

"No, no, no, Carter. You said something about an inspector. We're not really expecting an inspector this term, are we?"

Mr Carter pondered the query. A visit from one of HM Inspectors seemed to him unlikely, for it was not long since the Department of Education and Science had completed a full-scale inspection of the school. On the other hand, there was always the chance that one would decide to pay a call to see what progress had been made since his last visit. It was one of those things that was impossible to foretell.

"Well, I only hope he doesn't choose to come when I'm taking Form Three for history," Mr Wilkins said when his colleague had expressed his opinion. "I shan't forget the last time in a hurry. The inspector asked them a few simple questions about the work I'd been teaching them only the day before."

He shook his head as he recalled the complete and utter

silence that had followed the inspector's simple questions, with the class gaping blankly as though they had never been taught an historical fact in their lives. "It was terrible, Carter. I didn't know where to look. I felt I wanted to shout the answers out for them."

"Yes, I know that feeling," Mr Carter sympathised.

"And if I've to go through that horrible experience all over again I shall – I shall – well, let's hope I shan't have to!" At the risk of upsetting his teacup, Mr Wilkins rose to his feet and waved his hand in the air to emphasise his remarks. "Give me any other class in the school and I shall be delighted to entertain every inspector in the Department of Education and Science. But Form Three – well, I mean to say!"

"Stop worrying, Wilkins," Mr Carter advised. "I've just told you it's most unlikely we shall have a visit from them this term. I merely mentioned the matter to show that it was high time that Form Three pulled their socks up and got down to serious work."

"I'll see they do that. In fact, I've started on them already," Mr Wilkins replied. "I've set that boy Jennings so much history to learn in his spare time that he'll be able to write a book about Edward the First by this time next week."

In ones and twos the staff finished their tea and departed, and the room was almost empty when Matron made her way across to where Mr Carter and Mr Wilkins were still discussing the shortcomings of the third form.

"I've just discovered a secret," she told them with a smile. "It's Mr Hind's birthday on Monday."

The information evoked no enthusiasm in Mr Wilkins. "I don't call that much of a secret," he observed. "I should have thought it was time Hind gave up having birthdays.

He's getting too old for that sort of thing."

"Nonsense," Matron contradicted. "We're never too old for birthdays. Anyway, I thought it might be a good excuse for us to plan a little celebration."

"What sort of celebration?" Mr Wilkins asked doubtfully.

"Oh, nothing very much. Just a small coffee party here in the common room after the boys have gone to bed. Of course, we must keep it a secret from Mr Hind until the time arrives."

"It sounds a very good idea, Matron," Mr Carter said. "I'm sure we'll all enjoy it enormously – especially Wilkins. It'll help to take his mind off Form Three."

"Perhaps you're right," his colleague agreed. "Goodness knows I need something to cheer me up after coping with those silly little boys all day long." His mood changed for the better as he considered the idea more carefully. "I'll tell you what, Matron. You provide the coffee, and I'll slip down to the village in my car on Monday afternoon and order some cakes. How would it be if I got some of those sticky pink contraptions sprinkled with what-do-you-call-it? They always go down well. And perhaps a few of those creamy concoctions with jam in the middle?"

Matron smiled again as she turned to leave the room. "I should just order a dozen assorted and hope for the best," she advised. "And not a word to anyone, mind. Mr Hind's birthday party has to be a complete surprise."

It took Darbishire most of his spare time for the next two days to copy out the first six pages of Chapter Nine in his history book. Just before bedtime on Sunday he laid his pen down and sat back from the common-room table with a sigh of relief.

"Phew! Thank goodness, that's over!" he declared. "How are you getting on, Jen? Do you know it yet?"

Jennings shook his head in despair. Learning six pages by heart was a far more difficult matter than merely copying out the text from the book. For the last hour he had sat crouching forward in a doubled-up posture with the book on the floor between his feet: but so far he had been unable to commit more than a few lines to memory. He *must* get the first page right, he told himself severely. He would read it through once more and then ask Darbishire to test him. Frowning in concentration he mouthed each word silently as he read: *Edward I. 1272–1307. The reign of Edward I saw Parliament used for the first time in history as an instrument of government. It was during this reign that great reforms were made in legal matters, for it was Edward's aim to make the government of the country strong and bring the whole of the British Isles under one rule. . . .* Yes, he felt sure he knew that much by heart.

"Will you hear me, Darbi?" he asked.

Darbishire wiped his ink-stained spectacles with his inky fingers and peered intently at the text book on the table before him. "Get on with it then," he said.

"'The reign of Edward the First saw Parliament used for the first time in history as a' – as an implement or something . . ." Jennings began.

"Instrument, not implement. An instrument of government."

"Yes, that's right. 'It was during that reign . . .'"

"Hey! Whoa! Stop! You're off the beam," Darbishire broke in.

"No, I'm not. This is the bit I've learnt."

"You're wrong, anyway. It should be 'during *this* reign', not 'during *that* reign'."

"Oh, for goodness sake! What difference does that make?" Jennings complained.

"It makes a fantastic lot. Old Wilkie said you'd got to be word perfect, and if you say *that* instead of *this* he won't pass you."

Jennings clicked his tongue in reproach. "Don't be so fussy, Darbi. You'll be expecting me to put in all the commas and semi-colons next." He took a deep breath, closed his eyes and continued, "'It was during this reign that great reforms were made in legal matters, for it was Edward's aim to – er – to – er . . .' Oh fish-hooks! Don't breathe so loud, Darbi. You put me off!"

"That's a feeble excuse, if ever I heard one!" snorted the prompter. "Honestly, Jen, you're hopeless! You'd better have another bash at learning it in bed tonight, and I'll hear you tomorrow."

Just then, the common-room door swung open and Atkinson walked in. Having fully recovered from the effects of tonsilitis, he had been discharged from the sick-room and sent back to join his friends. He had enjoyed his convalescence so much that he had been hoping to prolong his stay for a further twenty-four hours, but unfortunately Matron had thwarted his plans by sending him back into school on Sunday evening in readiness for work the following morning.

"Hullo, you blokes," he greeted them. "What's been going on around these parts since I've been away?"

"Nothing much, really. Old Wilkie's been on the warpath once or twice," Jennings informed him. "He got a bit peeved because we found that guinea-pig, but he seems to be calming down a bit now."

It was news to Atkinson that Jennings and Darbishire had been involved in the misunderstanding over the missing guinea-pig. The only thing he had learnt from his grandmother was that he would find the pet awaiting him when he returned home for the Easter holidays.

"You'll have to call him F. J. Saunders, because that's the name we gave him," Jennings observed after they had spent a few minutes discussing the comings and goings of the elusive animal. A flicker of disappointment clouded his eyes as he added, "Of course, we didn't see enough of him to get to know him very well, what with Old Wilkie being on his track all the time, but he's a really nice pet, so mind you look after him properly."

In Dormitory Four that evening it was only natural that Atkinson's return should lead the conversation round to the subject of the postponed dormitory feast.

"You're a bright sort of specimen, Atki, I must say," Temple remarked as he screwed up his Sunday suit into a tight ball and squeezed it into his clothes locker. "All that guff about generously providing tins of Irish stew and stuff, and then you calmly waltz off to the sick-room and leave us stranded!"

"I couldn't help it – I was ill," Atkinson defended himself.

"We can still have the feast, now you've come back," Venables suggested. "I suppose your grandmother *did* bring the stew and stuff that you asked for?"

"Well, no; I did ask her to, but actually she brought a bottle of barley water and a guinea-pig instead."

"A fat lot of good that was!" snorted Temple. "Here we've been waiting all this time for you to provide the provender you promised, and now you calmly turn round and tell us you haven't got it."

"Well, if you'd been as ill as I was you wouldn't have . . ."

Venables intervened to point out that nothing would be gained by arguing. If the plans for the feast were to go ahead – and it was unthinkable that they should be abandoned now that the treat had been in store for so long – then they must fall back upon Jennings' original suggestion. Each must subscribe according to his means. Surely between the five of them they could raise enough for a simple, though satisfying meal.

"I've got a pound and two pence to start the ball rolling," volunteered Jennings.

"And I've got a pound postal order my uncle sent me last week," added Temple.

This was a promising start. And when, in addition, Darbishire promised to subscribe sixty pence, and Venables a further twenty pence, it was felt that the feast would not, after all, suffer from lack of funds. Atkinson had no money. Instead, he offered his services in any capacity in which they could be of use.

Venables totted up the total. "Two pounds, eighty-two! That'll be masses!" he crowed, hurling his pyjamas into the air in delight. By chance, the top half came to rest in a washbasin full of water, and he was obliged to spend the night wearing his shirt in place of his pyjama jacket.

"When shall we have the feast?" Darbishire asked, when Venables' sodden nightwear had been hung out of the window to dry.

"The sooner the better. If we put it off again old Atki will go beetling back to the sick-room with indigestion or housemaid's knee, or something," said Temple. "Why not tomorrow night? One of us could get permission to slip into the village after lunch, and then we can cook the stuff on the boiler during prep."

All eyes turned to Jennings. As he had suggested the

plan in the first place, it was clearly his duty to carry out the final arrangements. And yet, somewhat to their surprise, he seemed reluctant to play a leading part in the proceedings.

"I don't see how *I* can go in to Linbury. I've got another five pages of history to learn," he demurred. "And anyway, I've been in such a lot of trouble with Old Wilkie lately that I don't want to run into any more."

Eyebrows were raised in pained surprise.

"But you can't back out of it now," Temple protested. "It was you who was so really keen on the idea. It was you who found out that the masters were having furtive feasts in the staff-room. It was you who . . ."

"Yes, I know I did, but that was weeks ago. I haven't seen any more food being carted along there for ages."

"Perhaps they smuggle it in when no one's looking," Atkinson hazarded. "Go on, Jen; if you'll go and buy the stuff, I'll do the cooking. I've got an old biscuit tin I can use for a saucepan."

Jennings frowned in indecision. He had been in so much trouble the last few days that he was more than anxious, for the time being, to keep on the right side of the law. And yet, as the instigator of the feast, he could not withdraw just when events were approaching a climax.

"Oh, all right," he said grudgingly. "But when I'm going to find time to learn my history, I just don't know."

The next morning, during break, Jennings made out a shopping list.

Things to Have for Irish Stew he jotted down on the memoranda page of his diary. After that he wrote:

| Bacon | - | - | - | - | Some rashers |
| Sausages | - | - | - | - | Enough for five |

Onions	-	-	-	-	As many as poss.
Potatoes	-	-	-	-	About three each
Doughnuts	-	-	-	-	

He was just debating in his mind whether the doughnuts should be added to the main dish or eaten as a separate course, when the other members of his dormitory filed into the common room bearing their contributions.

Temple handed over his postal order with a flourish. It had been made out in his name and signed by him at the bottom in a properly legal manner. There was, however, one puzzling feature which Jennings queried at once.

"What's all this crossing out on the front of it?" he demanded suspiciously. "Someone's scribbled two lines right across it – in ink, too, so we can't rub them out."

"That's perfectly all right. My uncle's crossed it," Temple hastened to explain. "You're allowed to do that with postal orders. You can have them either crossed or uncrossed, just as you like."

"What's the point of that?"

Temple hunched his shoulders in a shrug of uncertainty. "Just to give you a choice, I suppose. I expect some people like their postal orders with crosses on them just as – well, like, say, for instance, just as other people prefer their tea with sugar in it."

Satisfied, Jennings slipped the contribution into his pocket. There was a post office counter in the village stores where he would be able to change the order for cash when he started his shopping. "Righto. Who's next?" he asked.

There came a clinking of glass as Venables set down four empty lemonade bottles on the common-room table.

"*Voilà!*" he exclaimed. "Five pence back on each bottle, and there's the twenty pence I promised you."

This was not the sort of contribution that Jennings had been expecting and he felt doubtful about accepting a donation in kind, instead of in cash. However, the donor assured him that he would not have the slightest difficulty in claiming the deposit payable on each bottle.

"Any shop that sells lemonade will give you five pence back on the bottle," Venables explained. "I brought these back at the beginning of term, and I've been saving the empties for a rainy day."

Lastly came a donation from Darbishire.

"Three brand new, twenty pence stamps to the value of sixty pence," he announced as he produced them from his writing-case. "They've got a bit creased, I'm afraid; and one of them's got a slight ink smudge, and one of the others hasn't got any sticky stuff on the back: but they're all right because they've never been used."

"They may not take stamps at the shop," Jennings demurred, eyeing the crumpled specimens with distaste.

"They're bound to. It's a post office as well, you know, so they'll probably be glad of them. It'll save them having to order some more quite so soon."

"All right, then," Jennings agreed. "Let's just check how much we've got. There's my pound and two pence in cash, a pound postal order, sixty pence in stamps and twenty pence in empty lemonade bottles. That's – er – um – Yes, that's right: it comes to two pounds, eighty-two, all told."

The total was received with wild acclaim.

"Fantastic! You'll be able to buy masses of Irish stew for that!" said Temple. "And you're going to cook it in the biscuit tin, aren't you, Atki?"

The chef smiled brightly to conceal the doubts that had been assailing him ever since his rash promise had been accepted. How did you set about making a stew? he wondered. And in what way did the Irish variety differ from any other? He could not ask Matron for fear of revealing their plans. These national dishes were all very confusing to a beginner: Irish stew, Welsh rabbit, Scotch eggs, French beans, German sausage. No wonder the best chefs were usually foreigners!

For half an hour after breakfast he had searched through the shelves of the school library for a cookery book, but he had not been able to find anything which was helpful in the slightest degree. The encyclopaedia which he had consulted, though devoting three pages to Irish history, had had nothing to say about Irish stew. However, he would manage somehow, he felt sure of that.

Aloud he said, "Yes, of course: you can leave all that side of it to me. Actually, I've never made Irish stew before, but I think I'll be able to fix it."

"It's dead easy," Venables told him. "All you've got to do is bung the ingredients in the biscuit tin, cover them with water and let them boil till they're done."

"And how long will that take?"

"I couldn't say. You'll just have to keep an eye on it. Of course, if you ram the lid of the biscuit tin down hard enough, you'll be able to make a home-made pressure cooker and then it'd be done in half the time."

The bell for the end of break put a stop to further discussion, and they all hurried off to their classroom, well-satisfied with their plans so far.

If the event was a success, they might even consider repeating the experiment at regular intervals. The possibilities were endless . . . Why, perhaps in the years to come, the *Dormitory Four Annual Dinner*, though strictly unofficial, might be looked upon by future generations as one of the most cherished traditions of Linbury Court School.

Chapter 12

Catering Arrangements

The school was lining up for lunch in the lobby outside the dining-room as Matron came downstairs from the dispensary to start serving out the first course. She exchanged a word with Mr Carter who, as master on duty, was holding a brief inspection to see that all hands had been washed and all hair neatly brushed in readiness for the meal.

Near at hand, Mr Wilkins was pinning up the football sides for the afternoon's games, and as Matron drew level with the noticeboard she said, "You won't forget those cakes you promised to bring to the coffee party this evening! There'll be only three or four of us, apart from Mr Hind, so I should think a mixed dozen of éclairs and fancy cakes will be enough."

Mr Wilkins turned away from the noticeboard frowning in self-reproach.

"Tut! As a matter of fact I *had* forgotten, Matron. I've been so busy over the weekend it completely slipped my mind."

"There's still time," she reminded him. "Couldn't you run down to the village in your car before afternoon school?"

"I'm afraid not. I took the alternator off during break because it wasn't working properly. I've mended it now, but it'll take me a little while to assemble it again. I was going to put it back after football this afternoon."

Matron's smile concealed her disappointment. "Never mind, Mr Wilkins; perhaps we can find someone else to go down to the village."

In her mind she ran over a list of possible shoppers. She herself would be busy all afternoon, and Mr Carter, as master on duty, would not be free to leave the premises. She could not very well ask Mr Hind to buy cakes for his own birthday party, for the affair was being planned as a surprise. Unless a substitute could be found, it seemed as though Mr Wilkins would have to postpone his alternator repairs and go into Linbury on foot.

Just then, Jennings stepped out of line and approached Mr Wilkins.

"Sir, please, sir, may I very kindly have per, sir, to go into . . ."

"May you have *per*?" echoed Mr Wilkins in disapproval.

"Sorry, sir. May I have permission, I should say, sir."

"So I should think. And whatever it is, ask Mr Carter. I'm not on duty."

Jennings looked round to find the duty-master standing just behind him.

"Sir, please, sir, may I go into the village before school this afternoon, sir?"

"Why?" Mr Carter asked.

Jennings hesitated. "I wanted to buy something to eat, sir."

"More tuck! That's all you boys ever think about," Mr Wilkins complained.

Mr Carter, however, was prepared to take a more lenient view, for the request was not an unusual one. The boys were allowed, at the duty-master's discretion, to buy things from the village shop.

"All right, then, Jennings. You can go immediately after

lunch, but mind you're back before the bell goes for school."

"Yes, sir. Thank you, sir."

As Jennings was about to resume his place in the line Mr Wilkins called him back.

"If you're going to the village you can do a little shopping for me, if you don't mind," he said. "I want you to buy me some cakes."

Cakes! Here was fresh evidence that Mr Wilkins was still indulging his whim for furtive feasting.

"You mean you want me to get you some to *eat*, sir?"

"Of course they're to eat! You don't imagine I want them to play ping-pong with, do you?"

"No, sir."

"Ask for a dozen assorted. I don't know how much they'll be," Mr Wilkins went on, producing three pounds from his pocket, "but this should be enough, I imagine."

"Yes, sir." Jennings pocketed the money. "I'll bring them back with me and take them up to your room, shall I, sir?"

Mr Carter had moved away to continue his inspection of hands and hair, but Matron was still listening to the arrangements.

"I think it would be wiser if you asked the shop to deliver them," she suggested. "I can just imagine what a bag of éclairs would look like after Jennings had trotted back from the village clasping them tightly in his arms."

"Or dropping them in a puddle every few yards," Mr Wilkins added. "Yes, you're quite right, Matron. I'll have them sent up, you hear, Jennings? Tell the shop to deliver them this afternoon as soon as they can. Don't try to bring them back yourself."

*　　*　　*　　*

As he hurried towards the village before afternoon school, Jennings tested himself on as much of his history punishment as he had committed to memory.

"'The reign of Edward the First saw Parliament used for the first time in history as an instrument of government,'" he announced to a bullock which was eyeing him solemnly from over a hedge . . . He'd never be able to learn it all by Friday, he told himself. Today was Monday, and so far he couldn't get to the bottom of the second page without a great deal of prompting.

"'. . . for Edward's aim was to make the government of the country strong and bring the whole of the British Isles under one rule,'" he informed a magpie perching on a telephone wire. "'In 1275 was passed' . . . Something or other." What on earth had happened in 1275? . . . Already he was floundering for words. And only four more days remained in which to become word perfect!

He was still trying to remember what had happened in 1275 when he reached the church at the end of the village street. From that point onwards he banished Edward the First from his mind and switched his train of thought to the purchases which he had to make.

There were three shops in the village of Linbury – H. Higgins, *Jeweller and Silversmith*; Chas. Lumley, *Home-made Cakes and Bicycles Repaired*; and the *Linbury Stores and Post Office*.

Of these, the last-named might almost be described as the commercial hub of the district, for it was here that the discerning shopper could buy a wide variety of goods ranging from mousetraps to moth balls, and bird seed to brussels sprouts.

He would do the bulk of his shopping at the Stores, Jennings decided, for they would be sure to have all the ingredients for a tasty Irish stew. First, however, he must cope with Mr Wilkins' order, and with this in mind he turned his steps towards the crudely-painted signboard advertising homemade cakes and cycling accessories farther along the street.

The catering department of the firm of Lumley (*High Class Teas a Speciality*) was carried on in the front parlour, for the premises could not be described as a shop in the true sense of the word. When Jennings entered, Mrs Lumley shuffled in from the kitchen in her bedroom slippers to attend to the needs of her customer.

"I've got some nice fancies here," she said in response to his query. "Eclairs, meringues, jam tarts and sponge with pink icing. Ever so nice, they are."

"It doesn't matter much what they taste like. They're for someone else, you see." After all, no one could expect him to take endless trouble about indulging an already over-fed schoolmaster! "I'll have a dozen mixed, please. Oh, and would you mind sending them? I don't want to take them with me."

Mrs Lumley took the money for the cakes, and said, "I'd better have your name and address, then."

"Whose – mine? My name's Jennings; J. C. T. Jennings, of Linbury Court School. The cakes aren't for me, though. They're for this other person I was telling you about."

"That'll be all right, then. I'll get my husband to bring them up to the school as soon as he comes in."

After her customer had left, Mrs Lumley selected twelve cakes and packed them in a box. All that remained was to write the instructions for delivery on the lid, so that the goods should not go astray. She remembered the address well enough, for the school was well-known in the village. What was the name, now? . . . Ah, she had it! Jennings, that was it. J. C. T. In clear bold letters she inscribed on the box: *URGENT. FRAGILE.* And underneath that: *J. C. T. Jennings, Linbury Court School.*

Once outside the Linbury Stores and Post Office, Jennings wasted no time. He made a beeline for the food counter where a young woman in an off-white overall was building a pyramid of tinned peas.

"Good afternoon. Do you sell Irish stew?" he inquired.

"Not ready mixed, we don't," she replied, breaking off from her building operations. "I dare say we've got all the things, though. What is it you want?"

Jennings fumbled in his pocket and produced the shopping list. . . Bacon, sausages, onions, potatoes; in a matter of minutes the ingredients of his choice had been assembled and weighed, and were ready to be packed up in a parcel. Everything, that is, except the doughnuts, which he had decided to leave until he knew whether or not he could afford a second course.

"How much does that come to, please?" the customer inquired. "I'd better know how much I've spent before I order any more."

The assistant added up the total. "That'll be two, seventy-five, so far."

"Oh, good. I can go up to two pounds, eighty-two, you see, provided you don't mind taking these lemonade bottles in part exchange."

There came the clinking of glass as he eased Venables' contributions from his raincoat pocket and set them down upon the counter with a confident smile.

The young lady examined the labels on the bottles and shook her head. "I can't take these ones, I'm afraid."

"Why not? There's five pence due back on each!"

"Not at this shop, there isn't," she explained. "We don't

sell this make of lemonade here, so we can't take the bottles back."

The confident smile vanished. This was a setback which he had not foreseen. Now he came to think of it, Venables had said something about bringing the lemonade back to school at the beginning of term. Obviously, he had bought them from a shop which stocked a different brand from that of the Linbury Stores and Post Office.

"Oh fish-hooks! That means I'm twenty pence down the drain. You'd better wipe out the onions," he said with a grimace. "Still, I shall be able to pay for the rest, when I've changed this postal order."

He moved away to the Post Office counter farther down the shop. But here a fresh disappointment awaited him. The man in charge glanced briefly at Temple's postal order and then handed it back.

"I can't change this for you. It's crossed."

"Yes, I know it is, but it's quite all right, all the same. One of the boys at school told me." What was it Temple had said?. . . Oh yes! "Some people like their postal orders crossed, just as other people like a lot of sugar in their tea – or something."

The sub-postmaster was not to be swayed by this argument. There was a hint of disapproval in his voice as he said, "I don't know what sugar in your tea has got to do with it, but I'll tell you this much." He pointed to the two ink lines drawn across the face of the order. "This means that the money's got to be paid through a bank. It can't be cashed in the ordinary way."

Jennings was aghast at the revelation. Why, Temple's pound was a vital contribution to the feasting fund. How could their plans succeed without it?

"This is gruesome. Couldn't I rub the lines out, or

scratch them off, or something?" he asked hopefully.

"You'd find yourself in trouble if you tried!"

"But what am I going to do, then?" Jennings demanded in despair. "First the lemonade bottles are no good, and now you say the postal order is a dud."

"I didn't say that. I said I couldn't accept it." The man's voice took on a more kindly tone as he added, "I'm sorry, son, but it's not my fault. I'm not allowed to cash crossed postal orders over the counter."

Worried now, Jennings produced the final contribution from his pocket.

"Well, anyway, these stamps will be all right, won't they?" he queried. "I mean, they're not crossed or anything."

"Stamps!"

The note of disapproval crept back into the sub-postmaster's voice. And this grew more pronounced as he noticed the ink blots and the shortage of gum on Darbishire's crumpled contribution.

"Listen, son. This is a General Stores and Post Office. We *sell* postage stamps – we don't buy them. Certainly not dirty-looking specimens in this condition."

"But they've never been used. You'd be able to sell them again ever so easily if you cleaned them up a bit and put some more sticky stuff on; and then you could ask for three less the next time you order some more."

His pleadings were in vain. The stamps were of no value as legal tender. With a heavy sigh he made his way back to the food counter to cancel half of his order.

After an earnest discussion with the young woman in the off-white overall, he decided to spend ninety pence on sausages and the remaining money on potatoes. Then, as time was growing short, he hurried back to school with the useless lemonade bottles clanking in his pocket and the food for the feast clasped tightly against his chest.

He'd have something to say to the others when he saw them, he reflected bitterly as he trotted along the Linbury road. A fine lot of contributions *they'd* raised between them . . . Worthless postal orders, bogus bottles, shop-soiled stamps. Why, if it hadn't been for his contribution in cash there just wouldn't *be* a dormitory feast at all!

The remainder of Dormitory Four were not seriously perturbed when told that their contributions had not been of any use. So long as they had boiled potatoes and sausages to look forward to, they were quite happy to forgo the rest of the ingredients. They were even happier to receive their donations back untouched, and paid scant attention to Jennings' complaints when he recounted all he had endured on their behalf.

"A bright bunch of clodpolls you are!" he fumed when they met shortly before tea to hear his news. "You and your contributions! I felt ever such a clueless clodpoll when they said your bottles were old junk and your postal order was a dud!"

"Well, never mind, we can still make a stew with the potatoes and sausages," Temple consoled him. "And I've managed to scrounge a few brussels sprouts, so we can bung those in as well."

"Where did you get them? Not out of the dustbin?" asked Darbishire with sudden suspicion.

"Oh, no! Old Bromo's been growing them in his garden plot, and he said we could have them when I told him what we were doing."

Atkinson, as chief cook, started his preparations in the tuck box room directly after tea. First, he scrubbed the potatoes with his nail brush and cut them into wafer thin slices with a razor blade he used for sharpening pencils. After that he dropped sausages, potatoes and sprouts into the biscuit tin and added a few drops of water. Then he crept unobserved into the boiler-room where he placed the makeshift casserole on top of the furnace.

When evening preparation was over, the boys took it in turns to visit the boiler-room at regular intervals to see what progress was being made. This called for a stealthy approach and could only be carried out when the master on duty was known to be occupied in some other part of the building.

At 7.35 Darbishire returned to the common room to announce that the stew was brewing nicely and giving off an aroma which could be smelled as far away as the shoelockers.

Ten minutes later Temple reported that the paint had blistered on the outside of the biscuit tin. In his opinion Atkinson had not used enough water, but he could not be sure about this without inspecting the contents more closely; and this, unfortunately was not possible as the tin was now too hot to handle.

At five minutes to eight Jennings sped down to the boiler-room for a final reconnaissance. He was gone some while, and had not put in an appearance when the dormitory bell sounded and the rest of the boys made ready to go upstairs to bed.

Darbishire and Venables discussed the coming banquet as they crossed the hall on their way to the main staircase.

"We'll have to hurry up and get into bed as fast as we can," Darbishire said anxiously. "We mustn't keep Mr Carter waiting when he comes to put the light out because we can't get cracking until he's gone downstairs to staff supper."

"What comes after that is the part I'm looking forward to," Venables replied, hopping from foot to foot with excitement. "Hooray for the famous furtive feast, fried in the furnace. I'm feeling famished!"

He broke off, surprised at the alliteration which had come so unexpectedly to his lips. "Hey, that was brilliant of me! Did you hear what I said, Darbi? All *f*'s. I said . . ."

"All right, all right, I heard!" There was a nervous edge on Darbishire's voice. Now that their plans were approaching the climax, he began to feel worried. "I can't think what old Jen's doing down in the boiler-room. I only hope to goodness . . ."

He was passing the hall table as he spoke, and his words died away as he caught sight of a square cardboard box lying upon it, bearing an inscription on the lid. *URGENT. FRAGILE*, it read.

Below that was a name and address in bold, clear letters: *J. C. T. Jennings, Linbury Court School.*

Chapter 13

No Smoke Without Fire

Darbishire stared at the cardboard box with growing wonder. If it was urgent it must be taken to the owner without delay. And if it was fragile . . . ! Curious to know what delicate object lay within, he eased open the lid.

"Crystallized cheesestraws! Look what I've found!" he cried, his eyes sparkling with delight. "Cakes! Eclairs, jam tarts, meringues – the lot! A whole dozen of them!"

Venables whistled in surprise. "Where did old Jennings get those from? And what did he want to go and leave them in the hall for?"

"They must be part of the feast," Darbishire reasoned. "A second course, perhaps, that he was going to keep under his hat till after we'd finished the stew."

"Under his hat!" It seemed a strange hiding-place for a dozen fancy cakes.

"Not really, you clodpoll. I mean he was going to keep it a secret."

"Oh, I see. That was crafty of him. And really great to plan a surprise like this. I reckon he must have had a lot more money tucked away to pay for this little lot."

"Well, of course. But he couldn't tell us, or that would have given the game away."

There was still no sign of Jennings so, for security reasons, Darbishire removed the box of cakes from the table and took it upstairs with him to Dormitory Four.

It would be asking for trouble, he decided, to leave such

telltale evidence in the hall where some member of the staff might come across it at any moment. Supposing Mr Wilkins were to find it on his way to the dining-hall! Darbishire shuddered at the thought and tucked the box beneath his blazer to shield it from prying eyes.

"Where can we put it while we get undressed?" Venables queried as they went upstairs. "There's nowhere safe to hide it in the dorm – especially with Mr Carter on duty. He's got electronic eyesight."

"You're telling me!" said Darbishire in worried tones. "It'd be better if we could leave it outside till after lights out." He brooded over the matter for a few moments and then his eyes lit up in inspiration.

On the landing, just outside the dormitory door, was a recess in the wall some eighteen inches wide. Here stood a fire extinguisher, one of many which were placed at strategic points about the building.

"We can bung it behind the extinguisher. No one will ever see it there," Darbishire decided, as he stooped to put his plan into operation.

The round metal cylinder provided adequate cover. Unless the extinguisher was moved bodily from the recess, no one could tell that a box of Mrs Lumley's special fancy cakes was concealed behind it.

Satisfied, the two boys hurried into the dormitory and began throwing off their clothes with feverish haste.

"We mustn't keep Mr Carter talking when he comes round," Venables informed Temple and Atkinson who were already in their pyjamas. "We've got to get rid of him as quickly as we can."

"Yes, of course. And it might be a good idea to yawn quite a lot. That'll show him we're in a hurry to get off to sleep," Atkinson suggested.

At that moment there came a scurry of feet on the landing and Jennings hurried into the room.

"Sorry I've been so long, you lot," he apologised. "Old Robo was sweeping up in the basement. I had to hang about till he'd pushed off, or he'd have seen me foxing into the boiler-room."

They nodded their heads in approval of these tactics. Robinson, the school cleaner, was well known for his habit of reporting suspicious behaviour to the master on duty.

"And how's the feast getting on?" asked Temple, concealing beneath his pillow the five plates of corrugated cardboard which he had made earlier in the day.

"It's done to a turn. If anything, it's gone round the bend a bit," Jennings announced as he scrambled out of his sweater. "All the water had boiled away when I got there. The sprouts and potatoes had, sort of, glued themselves to the bottom of the tin, and the sausages were going black."

"Black!" cried Atkinson aghast. "You mean they're ruined?"

"I wouldn't say that. They're only a sort of pale black at the moment, but we mustn't leave them much longer or they'll be frizzled to a cinder. They should be all right if we can get our light put out pretty quickly. Then, as soon as the coast's clear, I can fox down and bring up ye banquet."

"Goodo!" Darbishire approved. "And you needn't worry about the second course, Jen. Venables and I have attended to that."

"Second course! What second course?" Jennings demanded.

"You needn't pretend you don't know about it," Venables said with a grin. "Just as well we found it, though. You must be crazy leaving it about where everyone could see it. Especially with your name plastered all over it."

Jennings shook his head in perplexity. "I don't know what you're talking about."

"Don't be so thick," Darbishire remonstrated. "Venables and I were on our way up to bed and there, sitting on the hall table, was a . . ." He broke off in sudden panic as the tall figure of Mr Carter walked in through the open dormitory door.

"Who or what was sitting on the table, Darbishire?" the master inquired with interest.

"Nothing, sir. Nobody, sir. Or rather, nothing that really matters, sir," the boy replied uneasily.

It came as a welcome change to Mr Carter to find Dormitory Four hurrying so willingly to bed. He had never known them to wash so quickly and fold up their clothes with such speed. It was such an unusual sight that he stayed to watch; and his continued presence gave Darbishire no further chance to tell Jennings of his fateful discovery in the hall.

In a matter of minutes the five boys were all in bed. Temple emitted a loud, counterfeit yawn.

"My word, I'm tired. I shall be glad to get off to sleep," he announced with feigned weariness.

"Yes, so shall I," said Atkinson. "I think we're all ready for you to put the light out now, sir."

Mr Carter looked at him curiously. These were strange remarks from boys who normally spent their last waking moments bouncing up and down on their bedsprings. It looked suspiciously as though something was in the wind.

With slow, unhurried steps he paced the length of the dormitory three or four times, and then came to rest alongside the washbasins.

"Tut, tut! This wretched cold tap is dripping again," he observed. "I wonder if I could mend it."

140

"I shouldn't bother with it now, sir," Jennings urged. "Robinson could fix it in the morning."

"It's no bother, Jennings. I shouldn't like to think of your good night's rest being spoiled by a dripping tap," the master replied. "I'll fetch a spanner from the workshop and do it right away."

As he walked to the door, Mr Carter was aware of how tense the atmosphere had become. From the corner of his eye he noticed the panic-stricken glances which flashed from bed to bed. Clearly, they were anxious to be rid of him with all possible speed.

"I'll be back in a minute," he told them casually as he left the room.

Alarm and despondency spread round Dormitory Four as the duty master's footsteps died away along the landing.

"This is frantic," moaned Jennings. "If he's going to hang about in here doing odd jobs half the night, the feast will be ruined. There'll be nothing left but charred remains by the time he's finished."

"Couldn't you slip down and take it off the boiler?" urged Darbishire.

"How can I?" Jennings retorted. "I'd be bound to meet him on the stairs. It's a pity I didn't bring it with me when I came up to bed."

"A fat lot of good that would have done! He'd have smelled it in a flash," said Venables.

"What are we going to do, then?" Atkinson demanded. "If we leave it cooking much longer, the fumes will come wafting up the stairs and then we *shall* be in the soup."

"Not in the soup, Atki; in the stew," corrected Darbishire. "Or rather . . ."

"Ssh! Ssh! He's coming back!"

The sounds of urgent hushing were not lost upon Mr

Carter as he re-entered the room. As yet he did not know the nature of the plot that was so obviously due to hatch at any moment, but this did not worry him unduly . . . Time would tell: and he was in no hurry.

Wielding the spanner in a leisurely manner he began to tinker with the tap. Behind him the air of tension grew more and more strained.

"Will it take you very long, sir?" Jennings inquired after a few agonising seconds had ticked away.

"I really couldn't say. I may get it finished in ten minutes . . ."

"Ten minutes!" mouthed Darbishire in silent horror.

"On the other hand, it may take me half an hour or so." A sonorous buzzing then broke upon the air. Mr Carter was humming contentedly at his work.

A minute passed. Then Jennings sat bolt upright, sniffing the air cautiously like a stag scenting the hounds' approach. There was no doubt about it: an aroma was making its way up the stairs.

Darbishire, to the windward, was the next to catch the scent, and his nose twitched like a rabbit's as he tested the atmosphere.

"What's the matter with you two?" inquired Mr Carter, turning away from the basins. "Haven't you got a handkerchief?"

"Yes, sir. I thought I . . ." By this time it was futile to pretend that all was well with the ventilation. "I thought I smelled something, sir," Darbishire said with a gulp.

"Perhaps it's your supper, sir," suggested Venables. "Hadn't you better go and see, sir? I shouldn't like to think of your meal being spoiled just because of us, sir."

"That's all right. There's plenty of time," replied Mr Carter.

As he spoke, heavy footsteps could be heard thumping up the stairs and across the landing. A moment later, Mr Wilkins appeared on the threshold in a state of agitation.

"I say, Carter, something peculiar is going on," he panted. "I think the building's on fire."

Mr Carter refused to be ruffled by this announcement. "What's burning?" he inquired calmly.

"I don't know. But whatever it is, it's downstairs. There's a cloud of smoke billowing up from the basement. I've just come up for the extinguisher, and then I'm going down to investigate."

So saying, Mr Wilkins seized the fire extinguisher from its recess and charged off hot-foot to the basement to fight the flames.

Panic and dismay gripped the would-be feasters. Numb with shock they lay between the sheets, powerless to save the situation.

All except Jennings. Impulsively, he leaped out of bed and scurried barefooted in the wake of Mr Wilkins. It was too late to save the feast, but it might yet be possible to avert attention from the cause of the fire.

"Hey, where are you off to?" Mr Carter demanded as the boy shot out through the door.

"I'm going to help Mr Wilkins, sir. He may need someone to open the door for him, as he's carrying the extinguisher."

Jennings did not wait to hear Mr Carter's reply, but skidded pell-mell along the landing and raced down the stairs two at a time. At all costs he must catch up with Mr Wilkins before he reached the door of the boiler-room.

Upstairs in the dormitory, Mr Carter remained calm amidst the consternation. He had known false alarms in the past, caused by a sudden back-draught from the boiler wafting fumes of burning rubbish about the building. On this occasion he would wait for his colleague's report before issuing orders for fire drill.

He strolled out on to the landing and paused by the recess. His eyebrows rose as he noticed upon the floor a cardboard box, clearly visible now that the fire extinguisher had been taken away. Would this, perhaps, provide some clue as to why the boys had been so anxious to get rid of him? . . . He opened the lid and looked inside.

A moment later he returned to the dormitory with the box of cakes in his hand.

"This appears to belong to Jennings, judging from the name on the lid," he observed. "Do any of you others know anything about it?"

Temple and Atkinson looked blank. Venables stared fixedly at the ceiling. Darbishire twisted his fingers and clenched his toes in an agony of apprehension.

"Do *you*, Darbishire?" Mr Carter inquired.

"Well, yes, sir," the boy confessed. "They were just a few cakes that we were – sort of – going to – er – well . . ."

"That Jennings had provided for you to eat after lights out," Mr Carter construed. He shook his head sadly. "It's not as though you needed any more to eat. The school meals are perfectly adequate, surely!"

Darbishire hesitated. Mr Carter's last remark had awakened the sense of grievance they had felt when they had first planned the feast. Greatly daring he muttered, "*Some* people's are, yes, sir."

"What do you mean, Darbishire?"

It was too late to retreat. Awkwardly he stumbled on, "Well, sir, the real reason we decided to do it was because of the staff getting double meals, sir."

"You intrigue me, Darbishire. Who told you that?"

"Matron, sir. At least, she told Jennings she was taking extra lunches to the staff common room just after you'd had one in the dining-hall, sir."

Mr Carter blinked in surprise, utterly at a loss to understand this fantastic charge. "Tell me more," he said.

Darbishire did his best: but in the absence of the chief witness, the evidence – now a month old – was not entirely convincing. Mr Carter racked his brain and consulted his diary; and finally came upon a clue to the mystery in an entry for the last week of February.

"Light is beginning to dawn," he remarked. "Yes, Darbishire, you were right about the extra lunches, but they weren't for the staff. They were for the gentlemen who were auditing the school accounts."

The news was received in stunned silence. Then Temple murmured, "Tut! Just like Jennings to go and get everything in a twist."

"It's most unfortunate for all of you," the master went on. "Because whatever prompted you to do it, I am certainly not going to overlook this matter of eating after lights out. I shall punish the whole dormitory when Jennings returns to hear what I have to say."

They were not kept waiting for long. After ten seconds of uneasy silence, footsteps were heard approaching, and Mr Wilkins walked into the room after depositing the fire extinguisher in its rightful place. Behind him came Jennings wearing a smile of relief.

"It's all right, Carter – only a false alarm. I didn't need the extinguisher after all," Mr Wilkins explained. "It looks as though Robinson must have put some highly combustible rubbish on the furnace earlier this evening."

"You've no idea what it was?"

"I haven't a clue. It had all burnt away to a cinder by the time I got there. There was nothing left but a red-hot tin and a smell like smouldering leather."

Dormitory Four breathed again. At least *one* of their two courses had escaped detection!

"Just as well you sent a boy down to help me, Carter," Mr Wilkins went on as Jennings jumped into bed. "I needed someone to hold the boiler-room door open when I went in to investigate."

Mr Carter nodded briefly and turned to where the latest arrival was snuggling down between the sheets.

"A word with you, Jennings," he said. "Darbishire informs me that you were proposing to share these cakes round the dormitory after lights out."

Jennings sat upright in surprise. "Oh no, sir," he protested as he caught sight of the box in the master's hand.

"You did buy these cakes, didn't you? Your name's on the lid clearly enough."

"Yes, that's right, sir. But I didn't buy them for *us*. They're for Mr Wilkins, sir. He told me to get them, honestly, sir."

At the mention of his name, Mr Wilkins turned to inspect the evidence.

"He's quite right, Carter. These cakes don't belong to him. They're the ones I asked him to order in the village – for our little celebration, you know. Good job you found them. I was wondering what had happened to them."

Mr Carter pondered this new aspect of the matter. It was possible that Darbishire's muddleheaded thinking had led him to jump to the wrong conclusion. On the other hand, there seemed to be more to this business than met the eye. Perhaps it would be better not to inquire too deeply, but to let sleeping dogs lie. Aloud he said, "This puts things in rather a different light. I can't very well punish the dormitory for eating cakes after lights out, now I find they would never have been given the chance to do so." He suppressed a smile as he added, "And I don't know what you were thinking of Darbishire, but you were certainly barking up the wrong tree if you imagined these cakes were for you."

"Yes, sir. No, sir. Thank you very much, sir," Darbishire mumbled, thankful to have escaped so lightly.

The dormitory light clicked off and the masters departed for their coffee party in the staff-room. As their footsteps died away along the landing, Venables uttered a long-drawn sigh.

"What a frantic bish," he complained. "What a ghastly catastroscope! When we came up to bed we'd got both Irish stew *and* cakes to look forward to, and now we've got nothing. Not a sausage!"

"It's all Jennings' fault," grumbled Temple. "Stuffing us with all that gobbledegook about the staff being furtive feasters, and they don't even get any more than we do."

"They don't?" Jennings' tone was incredulous.

"No, they certainly don't. Mr Carter said so."

There was a pause while this sank in. Then Jennings said, "Ah, but they've got those cakes, haven't they? Just think of them down there in the staff common room tucking into luscious meringues and things while we lie here in the darkness, tightening our belts . . ."

"We're not wearing belts," Atkinson pointed out.

"Well, tightening our pyjama cords, then, and wondering

if we can last out till breakfast time."

He tailed off into silence. It must be wonderful to be grown up, he thought. You could eat all day and all night if you wanted to, and nobody would ever say a thing!

Chapter 14

An Inspector Calls

By tea-time on Tuesday, Jennings could recite, without faltering, the first two pages of his history imposition. Twenty-four hours later he had memorised a further page and a half; and during the rest period in the library on Thursday, when Darbishire offered to test him, he was able to reach the bottom of page five. Only towards the end of the last paragraph did he require a certain amount of prompting.

"'. . . for as a result of the Model Parliament of 1295 the three estates of Clergy, Lords and Commons were fully represented.' *Phew*!" He paused for breath. "'At this time Edward was at war with France as he was a vassal of the French King for the – er –' for the *something* of Gascony."

"Want a prompt?" asked Darbishire with his eyes on the text.

"No, it's on the tip of my tongue. What's the word? Something like burglar. *Fief*, that's it . . . 'as he was a vassal of the French King for the fief of Gascony.'"

"A fief isn't a burglar, you clodpoll!" Darbishire said severely. "This is *F*-i-e-f – not *TH*-i-e-f!"

"Same thing," Jennings returned airily. "Some people can't say their *Th*'s very well. Perhaps Edward the First was one of them."

The prompter clicked his tongue in rebuke. "You're

crazy. They wouldn't put a thing like that in the history book, even if he was!"

"Why not? It says he was tall and fair-haired with long legs, so why shouldn't it say he always said *fief* instead of *thief*?"

Darbishire was trying to find the flaw in this reasoning when Mr Carter came into the library in search of Venables who had a dental appointment that afternoon in Dunhambury.

"Please, sir, will you settle an argument, sir?" Darbishire inquired politely, as Mr Carter paused by the library table. "Jennings seems to think that Edward the thirst was a fief – I mean that Edward the First was a thief."

"I didn't say that, sir," Jennings objected. "Darbishire's got it all wrong. I only said he couldn't sound his *Th*'s. And I ought to know, sir, because I've learnt five pages about him off by heart, and I shall know even more by this time tomorrow. Like to hear me say the next bit, Darbi?"

"Righto, Jen. You listen, sir; he's really good."

"'The Scots then made an alliance with the French . . .'"

The argument seemed to have been sidetracked without Mr Carter being called upon for his decision. As he moved away the sound of oratory grew fainter behind him.

"'. . . and Edward marched northwards to invade Scotland. On the 30th March, 1296, he took the town of Berwick-on-Tweed.'"

Venables had spotted Mr Carter by this time and came hurrying towards him.

"Please, sir, I've got to go to the dentist, sir. Matron said I'd got to clean my teeth and tell you I was catching the half-past two bus, and would you give me my fare, please, sir?"

Mr Carter nodded. "That's what I've come to see you about. Mr Wilkins is going in to Dunhambury by car in a few minutes, and he's kindly offered to give you a lift."

"Oh, good!" Venables brightened visibly. A ride in a master's car would make him the envy of his friends for days to come. "Will he be bringing me back to, sir?"

"No. He won't be returning until after tea, so you'll have to catch the four o'clock bus back to school."

"Yes, sir. What about my ticket, sir?"

"You'll need a half fare single to Linbury," said Mr Carter as he handed over the money. "Run along, now. Don't keep Mr Wilkins waiting."

The journey to Dunhambury was uneventful. Mr Wilkins' car was running well now that the alternator had been repaired. Ten minutes after leaving the school gates they drew up at the town centre, some five miles distant, and parked the car in the High Street facing the Town Hall.

Shortly after that two things happened which had some bearing on future events. The first occurred when Mr Wilkins returned to his car after seeing Venables to the dentist, and found a policeman standing beside it.

"Are you the owner of this vehicle?" the constable demanded, producing a notebook from his pocket.

Mr Wilkins admitted the fact. "Yes, that's right. There's nothing wrong, is there?"

The policeman indicated a metal plaque affixed to a nearby lamp-post.

"Just in case it has escaped your attention you happen to be parked on a yellow line," he said in the dull, resigned tones of a man who had already wasted the best part of the day dealing with erring motorists.

"Eh! Good gracious, so I am," Mr Wilkins exclaimed in dismay. "I'll move the car at once."

"It's a bit late for that now. You've been parked here long enough to obstruct the traffic."

Mr Wilkins apologised profusely. It was careless of him not to have seen the notice, he said, and he hoped that he had not caused any inconvenience to the cars and bicycles that were crawling along the High Street in a leisurely fashion.

"What I mean is, you – er – you're not going to issue a summons about this, are you, officer?" he finished up hopefully.

The policeman stroked his chin thoughtfully and refused to commit himself.

"You wouldn't be the first one I've reported today," he said. Whereupon he replaced his notebook in his pocket and stood watching as the offending motorist drove away in search of a lawful parking place.

The encounter with the policeman unsettled Mr Wilkins for the rest of the afternoon. He was annoyed with himself for so thoughtlessly parking on a yellow line; but what worried him more was the uncertainty of not knowing whether the matter would result in a summons. The constable had given no clue of his intentions. Was it safe to assume that he meant to let the matter drop?

In point of fact, such proved to be the case, but, as Mr Wilkins had no means of knowing this, he continued to feel vaguely uneasy. After all, he told himself, one could never tell what the outcome might be.

An hour later, Venables caught the four o'clock bus back to Linbury after his visit to the dentist. He asked for a half-fare single ticket and proffered the money which Mr Carter had given him for the purpose.

"*Half* single! And how old might you be?" asked the conductor, eyeing him with suspicion.

"Me? I'm only twelve – honestly I am."

The conductor added a wan smile to his look of disbelief.

He'd been collecting fares for too long to be deceived by fairy tales of that sort, his expresssion seemed to suggest.

"I've heard that one before," he said. "You don't expect me to believe that a lad your size is under fourteen, do you?"

"But I *am*. I'm not even thirteen till next month. I'm tall for my age, that's why."

It was clear that the conductor did not believe him for he held out his hand for the balance of the fare.

"I haven't got any more money, anyway, so you'll have to let me go for half," Venables protested. "And it's quite true about my being twelve. You ask anyone at Linbury Court School – ask the headmaster if you like!"

"It's not for me to go traipsing round finding out how old people are. It's the inspector's job to make inquiries if he's not satisfied." With bad grace the conductor punched a half-fare ticket and dropped the money into his leather pouch. "There's too many people getting away without paying the proper fare, if you ask me. Time it was put a stop to."

Though Venables' conscience was clear he was distressed by the injustice of the charge. "You mean you're going to report me to the inspector?" he asked.

"That's as maybe," the conductor mumbled as he returned to the rear platform of the bus. It was the end of the matter so far as he was concerned, but he did not see why he should go to the trouble of setting his passenger's mind at rest. It would do him good to keep him guessing for a bit. In arguments with members of the public, the conductor always liked to have the last word.

For the rest of the journey Venables debated in his mind how he could prove his innocence; and when he arrived back at school he had a word with Mr Carter whom he met leaving Form Five classroom at the end of the first lesson.

"Please, sir, have I got a birth certificate, sir?" Venables inquired anxiously.

Mr Carter looked surprised. "Yes, of course you have. I don't know where it is, but you're bound to have one somewhere. Why do you ask?"

"Well, I may need it, sir, because of being tall for my age." Venables' tone was solemn as he recounted the argument he had had on the bus.

". . . so if he *does* report me, sir, I thought I'd send them my birth certificate so they'd be able to see I wasn't trying to swindle them, sir."

Mr Carter refused to treat the matter seriously. "I don't think that will be necessary, Venables. It's most unlikely that you'll hear any more about it. And in any case, I can vouch for your age if any inquiries should be made."

"Thank you, sir. Thank you very much, sir." Relieved in mind, Venables scurried off to his classroom as the bell rang for the second lesson of the afternoon.

The weather turned wet the following morning, and at lunch time the headmaster announced that there would be no football during the afternoon. Accordingly, when the rest period was over, the boys settled down to a variety of indoor occupations.

Bromwich and Rumbelow played table tennis; Thompson and Nuttall played chess; Binns and Blotwell conducted an ear-splitting practice of the percussion band; and Martin-Jones whiled away the time flicking pellets of inky paper at anyone who came within range.

Jennings settled down in the library for a last-minute rehearsal of his imposition . . . *The reign of Edward I saw Parliament used for the first time in history as an instrument of government* . . . By now he felt confident that he could recite the six pages without being prompted, and was almost looking forward to the first lesson of the afternoon when he would be called upon to demonstrate his feat of memory. All the same, he reflected, it would do no harm to run through the text once more, just to make sure . . . *In 1297 the Scots rose in rebellion, but in the following year Edward invaded Scotland and defeated Wallace at the Battle of Falkirk* . . .

At twenty minutes to three Mr Carter was alone in the staff common room when a knock sounded on the door. It opened, at his bidding, and Darbishire sidled into the room.

In a loud, self-conscious whisper he announced, "Please, sir, there's a strange man in the hall, sir. He asked me to go and tell the Head or someone that he'd arrived, sir."

"I don't think the headmaster is available at the moment," replied Mr Carter. "Perhaps I'd better see who it is. Ask him to come in, will you, and then you can run along."

"Yes, sir."

There came an inaudible muttering from beyond the door and then a tall, upright gentleman in rimless glasses, wearing a dark overcoat and carrying a despatch case, came into the room.

"Good afternoon. My name is Macready," he said in slow, deliberate accents. "I'm from the Department of Education and Science. I'm an inspector of schools."

"How do you do?" Mr Carter said in a welcoming tone. "I wasn't expecting you. The Head didn't tell me you were coming."

"I gave him rather short notice, I'm afraid," Mr Macready explained as he divested himself of his overcoat.

"Ah, yes, of course; that might account for it." The headmaster had returned to Linbury only that morning after spending a few days in London. Clearly, he had not yet dealt with all the letters which had arrived during his absence.

"This isn't a very formal visit, you understand," the inspector continued. "I've come merely to verify one or two points arising from the full-scale inspection that some of my colleagues carried out some months ago."

"Quite. Well now, if you'll wait a few minutes I'll go and find the headmaster and tell him you're here." At the door Mr Carter turned and added, "Please make yourself comfortable. Perhaps you'd care to read the paper while you're waiting?"

But Mr Macready was already examining a stack of magazines on the staff-room table.

"Thank you, but I see you have the current number of the *Historical Review*. I'll read that if I may. History is my subject, you know – my special subject."

"Really!" said Mr Carter politely. He'd have to tell Mr Wilkins about this, particularly as history with Form Three would be his colleague's first lesson of the afternoon. The two historians might find much in common! . . . And Matron, too, would be interested to know of Mr Macready's visit in case he should wish to inspect some detail of the domestic arrangements.

As he closed the staff-room door behind him, Mr Carter caught sight of Darbishire and Atkinson, deep in conversation farther along the corridor.

"Come here, you boys," he called.

"You want us, sir?" they inquired in unison, skidding to a halt before him.

"Yes, I do. Darbishire, I want you to go and find Mr

Wilkins. Tell him an inspector has arrived and that he may be receiving a visit from him during the afternoon."

Darbishire's eyes shone with excitement. "An inspector! Wow!" he gasped.

"I beg your pardon, Darbishire?"

"Sorry, sir. I mean, yes, of course, I'll go and tell Mr Wilkins at once, sir."

As Darbishire scampered away on his errand, Mr Carter turned to his second messenger. "You'd better go and tell Matron, Atkinson. It's quite likely that the inspector will want to have a look round the building."

Atkinson looked vaguely worried. "Have I got to go and tell her myself, personally, do you mean, sir? You see, Mr Hind said I could do an extra music practice as it's wet this afternoon, and I was just going up to . . ."

"All right, then; find somebody else to take the message, but see it's done at once," Mr Carter broke in as he started to move away along the corridor. He really couldn't waste time listening to Atkinson's long-winded explanations with the headmaster still unaware that an important visitor was waiting to see him.

It did not take Atkinson long to find a substitute. Rounding a corner on his way up to the music room, he cannoned into Temple groping his way in the opposite direction with his eyes tight shut and twirling a football sock round and round like a propeller.

"Mind out, you clumsy clodpoll!" said Temple, opening his eyes. "I'm trying to navigate an aircraft by dead reckoning, and now you've gone and bumped me off course."

"Sorry," Atkinson apologised. "Are you just zooming about, or flying anywhere special?"

"Well, actually I was trying to get all the way up to

Matron's room without looking." Temple held the makeshift propeller up for Atkinson's inspection. "I've got a massive great potato in the heel and she said she'd mend it if I brought it along."

"Goodo! You might give her a message when you get there. Tell her an inspector-bloke has rolled up and Mr Carter thinks she ought to know. I'd go myself, only I've got a music practice."

Temple pursed his lips, deciding whether he should condescend to perform this gracious favour. Then he said, "Oh, all right. What sort of an inspector is he, in case she asks?"

"I don't know," Atkinson confessed. "Mr Carter didn't say."

"There's lots of different kinds you know," Temple pointed out. "You can have, like, for instance, inspectors of weights and measures, and cruelty to animals and income tax, or even sanitary inspectors."

"Yes, I expect that's what he is," said Atkinson, who had little interest in which category the visitor should be placed.

"He can't be all of them: that'd be crazy," Temple went on, warming to his theme. "For all you know he's not one of that lot at all. He may even have come to – er – let's see now . . ."

Temple searched his mind for yet another example of this all-embracing profession. "He's probably come to inspect the gas-meter, or something."

This wild speculation seemed as good a guess as any to Atkinson, who was not keen to prolong the discussion. "Yes, of course. I'd forgotten gas-meter inspectors. That must be who he is," he said.

Satisfied, Temple trotted off upstairs on his mission,

twirling his sock before his face and warbling his tidings to all and sundry in a shrill treble. The tune was that of "My Bonny": the words were entirely his own:

> "*The gas man has come to see Matron,*" he sang,
> "*To see Matron the gas man has come.*
> *The gas man has come to see Matron,*
> *Oh, rummity-tummity-tum!*"

Chapter 15

Confusion Below Stairs

The strains of song reached the ear of Venables as he pranced out of the junior common room and saw Atkinson standing in the corridor.

"Who's making that ghastly shemozzle? Sounds like a corncrake with laryngitis," he observed.

"It's only Temple going up to Matron," Atkinson explained. "I was telling him about an inspector-bloke who's just rolled up and he's gone to . . ."

"*Wow!*" The word shot from Venables' lips with a sound like an air gun discharging a pellet. "*What* did you say then? *Who* did you say had come?"

"An inspector," repeated Atkinson, puzzled at the violent reaction to his news bulletin.

"Fossilized fish-hooks! Come here, to the school!" Venables appeared to be in the grip of some strong emotion. "I bet I know what he wants, too. He's come to see my birth certificate."

Atkinson stared at him in bewilderment. "You must be crazy!" he said severely. "What makes you think the gas man wants to see your birth certificate?"

"You said he was an inspector."

"So he is. Mr Carter said so. It was old Temple who thought he might be the gas man."

"Well, he's wrong, then," Venables decided from his superior knowledge of the circumstances. "Just like old

Temple to go and get everything in a twist. That bloke's a bus inspector. He must be. It all fits in."

"What all fits in? What are you waffling about?"

From the puzzled expression on his face it was clear that Atkinson was at a loss to understand his friend's concern. So without more ado Venables outlined the events leading up to his altercation with the bus conductor the previous afternoon.

". . . and he wouldn't believe I was only twelve, and he threatened to report me to the inspector for not paying the full fare," he finished up.

Atkinson was agog with excitement. Here was something to break the tedium of a wet afternoon. "So you think they've got on your scent and tracked you down?"

"Must have. I told him which school I went to, you see. Still," Venables gave a little shrug of indifference, "I'm not worried, though. Mr Carter said he'd tell them it was all right."

The news that Mr Carter was last seen heading for Mr Pemberton-Oakes' study and might not be readily available caused Venables a qualm of uneasiness. In the absence of his birth certificate it was essential that he should be able to produce a reliable witness to speak on his behalf.

"Isn't there any other way you can prove how old you are?" Atkinson queried when he heard of this new source of anxiety.

"Well, there's my diary, of course," Venables replied after some thought. "It's got all my particulars in there. Name, age, size in shoes, telephone number, business address, if any – the lot."

"Well, there you are, then. That'd do just as well. I should find the inspector-bloke and show him. He'll feel an awful fool when he realises how young you really are."

"Righto! Come with me, then, to back me up in case he won't believe me."

The invitation banished all thoughts of music practice from Atkinson's mind. Whatever happened, he was determined to be amongst those present when Venables and his accuser met face to face.

In feverish haste the two scuttled off to their classroom to fetch the vital diary from Venables' desk.

Meanwhile, Darbishire was having some difficulty in finding Mr Wilkins. There was no answer when he knocked at the door of the master's room, and a search of lobbies and classrooms failed to reveal his presence.

There was no sign of him in the library, either, when Darbishire put his head round the door.

But Jennings was there, revising his history. He looked up when the door opened and beckoned his friend into the room.

"I can't stop. I'm on an urgent mission," Darbishire explained. "Something rather peculiar is going on."

"I bet it's not so peculiar as this history," Jennings retorted. "It says here on the last page: 'With his dying breath Edward charged his son.' Do you think he rushed at him like a bull at a gate and dropped down dead after the collision?"

Darbishire came into the room and glanced at the open history book on the table. "Don't be a clodpoll, Jen. That's not the end of the sentence. It means he charged his son not to bury his bones until Scotland was subdued."

"Oh, I see. I wondered how the bit about the bones fitted in." Jennings replied. "I know it all now, Darbi. Would you like to hear me say it?"

"Not at the moment, I wouldn't. I've got to find Old Wilkie. There's an inspector come specially to see him."

At once, Jennings forgot all about the dying moments of Edward the First.

"An inspector! Wow! Are you sure?"

"Yes, I was the first person to see him," Darbishire answered with pride. "I told Mr Carter he'd arrived."

"Was he in a police car?"

"Who? Mr Carter?"

"No, the inspector, you clodpoll!"

"Oh, I see." Darbishire had no precise information on this point, not having seen the visitor until he reached the hall. However, he was able to state, without hesitation, that the official was not wearing uniform.

"A plain-clothes inspector! Wow! That's pretty serious!" Jennings exclaimed when he had digested this information. "If it had been something simple like, say, for instance, not having a gun licence, they'd have just sent an ordinary policeman."

"But Old Wilkie hasn't got a gun," Darbishire objected.

"That proves what I said. It must be something so serious that they need a top-ranking, plain-clothes police officer to carry out an investigation. I wonder what Old Wilkie's been up to?"

It was, perhaps, unfortunate that Jennings had not been present in the corridor to hear Temple discoursing on the fact that there are many different kinds of inspectors; for he might then have reasoned that, as the term can be applied to members of widely differing occupations, it is always advisable to make sure what an inspector has come to inspect.

As it was, Jennings did not bother to reason anything of the sort. His mind leaped impulsively to the most exciting conclusion he could think of. Not for one moment did it occur to him that the visitor could be anything but an inspector of police. In fact, his mind was so strongly made up on this point that Darbishire did not think of questioning the opinion of his strong-willed friend. What was crystal clear to Jennings was clear enough for his right-hand man.

Jennings slammed shut the history book and jumped to his feet. He had no idea what the visit portended, but whatever it was he was not going to miss it.

"Come on, then, Darbi, I'll help you find him," he said, scurrying to the door. "And hurry up! It doesn't do to keep the police waiting, you know."

As they scuttled off on their search, Darbishire speculated on the possible results of the inspector's visit. Would Mr Wilkins be taken away in a police car, he wondered? Not that he bore him any ill-will, but the prospect of a free lesson with no master to take charge of the class was certainly something to look forward to.

"It's not much help to *me* if Old Wilkie's not there for history," Jennings said when Darbishire mentioned this possibility. "I've gone and learned all those six pages by heart now, don't forget. If only they'd had the gumption to arrest him last week, before I'd worn my brain down to the roots trying to remember it all, there'd have been some sense in it."

"I never said they were going to arrest him," Darbishire objected. "I only thought they might take him away to be an important witness, or something."

They had reached Form Five B's classroom by this time, and Jennings glanced in through the open door. To his delight, he saw Mr Wilkins alone in the room chalking up geometrical figures on the blackboard in readiness for evening prep.

"Sir! . . . Sir! . . . Oh there you are, sir," Jennings called as he bounced in through the door.

"What is it?" From his tone it seemed that Mr Wilkins was not pleased at the interruption. He continued drawing isosceles triangles without turning his head away from the board.

"Urgent message for you, sir, from Mr Carter," Jennings burst out. "There's a policeman to see you."

"*What!*"

The chalk emitted a grating squeak and the base of an isosceles triangle shot off the edge of the blackboard as Mr Wilkins wheeled round in sudden concern. "A policeman?" he echoed.

"Yes, sir. A plain-clothes officer, and Mr Carter says you're wanted, sir."

"I – I – Good heavens!" Mr Wilkins seemed strangely affected by the announcement. He pursed his lips and muttered, "Tut! So he *did* take my number after all."

It had been Darbishire's dearest wish to proclaim the shattering news item himself, and he felt distinctly annoyed with Jennings for stealing his thunder in this flagrant fashion. After all, was it not he, C. E. J. Darbishire in person, who had been selected for this confidential task?

With an air of anxious importance he asked, "Does that mean that you'll be – er – I mean, do you know what he wants you for, sir?"

Mr Wilkins nodded briefly. He could guess! In point of fact he had not seriously thought that his parking offence would lead to a summons. Apparently, he had been mistaken!

"Will you have to go off to the police station right away, sir?" Darbishire asked hopefully. "Or will you be here for history?"

"Of course I shall be here for history, you silly little boy!" Mr Wilkins said testily. "To hear you talk, anyone would think I was on the point of being clapped into handcuffs and driven away in a Black Maria."

"Sorry, sir. I only thought – I mean, as the officer was a plain-clothes one I wondered . . ." Darbishire lapsed into silence at the sight of Mr Wilkins' expression.

"Where is he? I'll go and see him at once," the master decided. He would explain what had happened; how, owing to a momentary lapse of attention, he had chanced to park on a yellow line. It was the sort of thing that might happen to anyone. Surely, if the inspector was a reasonable man he would agree to take no further action!

"I don't know where he is now, sir, but he was in the staff common room a little while ago," Darbishire volunteered. "We'll come with you if you like, and . . ."

"You'll do nothing of the sort, thanks very much!" came the curt reply.

This was a disappointment. "What do you want us to do then, sir?"

"*Do?* I don't mind what you do. Go and play tiddly-winks in the games room, or whatever you were doing before. I'm not having you boys hanging about, gawping like half-wits, while I'm talking to the inspector."

And Mr Wilkins strode from the room, rehearsing a few well-chosen phrases with which to clear up the misunderstanding and establish friendly relations with the officer of the law.

Michael Denis Macready, MA (Lond), was an earnest young man in his late twenties, who carried out his duties in a thorough and painstaking manner. Amongst his colleagues he was noted for the tact and patience which he exercised when dealing with shy and diffident pupils, and he took pride in the fact that he never allowed himself to become ruffled when confronted with some unexpected situation . . . But then, he had never before been to Linbury Court!

For some minutes he sat in the staff-room thumbing through the pages of the *Historical Review*. Then there was a knock at the door and a stockily-built boy came into the room.

"Good afternoon, young man. And what is your name?" Mr Macready inquired in kindly tones to put the boy at his ease.

"Please, my name's Temple. Matron told me to come and find you – that is, if you are the – er . . ." Temple paused. The visitor didn't fit in with his idea of what an official from the Gas Board should look like. Shouldn't he be carrying a large book in which to record the readings on the meter? . . . Perhaps he kept it in the shiny leather despatch case lying on the table.

However, his doubts were removed when the earnest young man rose and said, "Yes, I'm the inspector, if that's whom you're looking for. I suppose you've come to take me along to the headmaster?"

"Well, no, not exactly," Temple said as he shepherded the visitor out into the corridor. "Matron said I was to take you down to the basement. That's where the meters are, you know."

"The basement!" Mr Macready was puzzled. It was the schoolwork, not the premises, that he had come to inspect. However! Doubtless the headmaster would explain.

With a light step he followed his guide along the corridor and down a flight of stairs.

"It's rather dark at the bottom where the meters are,"

Temple informed him. "Have you got a torch?"

"A torch! No, I certainly haven't." Where on earth was the boy leading him? And what was this reference to meters?

"I should have thought you'd have brought one with you if you have to do a lot of poking about in dark cupboards and places," Temple observed as they descended the stairs. Anxious to display a technical interest he rambled on, "I suppose we must use a lot of gas in a school like this. How many terms per therm . . ." No, that wasn't quite right. "How many therms per term would you say we got through, roughly?"

"My dear boy, I haven't the slightest idea."

They had reached the bottom of the stairs by this time. The light was certainly dim and Mr Macready peered doubtfully into the surrounding gloom.

"Are you quite sure you're taking me the right way?" he demanded. "I cannot for the life of me understand why the headmaster should wish to receive me in the basement."

"Oh no! The Head's not here!" Temple laughed at the absurdity of such an idea. "The only thing you'll find around these parts are the meters. Matron said I was to bring you down and then leave you to find your own way up again."

Mr Macready's feelings were outraged. Never in the course of his career had he met with such discourtesy. He was about to protest in the strongest possible terms when there was a pounding of feet on the staircase behind him and two more boys clattered down into the gloom.

"Excuse me – I say – just a minute, please. Are you the inspector?" the taller of the two asked anxiously.

"I certainly am," Mr Macready replied curtly.

"Oh goodo! Well, I've brought you my diary so you can

see for yourself how old I am. I know I look a bit more but that's because I'm tall for my age!"

"Eh! What? I don't understand."

A small pocket diary was thrust under the inspector's nose, and in the dim light of the basement he found himself straining to read some badly scrawled jottings of personal memoranda.

Name – G. Venables, it ran.

Age last birthday 12 years.

"There you are, you see. Just above where it says '*Size in shoes – 5. Business address* blank'," Venables said earnestly. "And Atkinson will back me up if you don't believe me, won't you, Atki?"

The other boy nodded in assent. "Yes, rather. He's quite entitled to go for half price, really he is."

"Yes, but what *is* all this?" Mr Macready demanded in blank bewilderment. "What's going at half price? I don't want any size 5 shoes at any price!"

"That's all right, I'm not trying to sell you any," Venables explained. "I'm just showing you my diary because of the argument I had with one of your blokes on the bus yesterday."

"I haven't got any blokes – or any buses!" the visitor protested. Really, this was all most irregular. Were the boys off their heads, he wondered! He handed back the book and said in tones of strong disapproval, "Kindly stand out of my way. I haven't the faintest idea what you're talking about."

It was Venables' turn to look surprised. "You haven't? But you must have, if you've come about my travelling at half fare. You – er – you *are* the bus inspector, aren't you?"

"Well, upon my soul! I've never heard such a . . ." The

words tailed off into scandalised muttering. Mr Macready was rapidly losing the unruffled calm on which he prided himself so keenly.

"You've got it all wrong, Venables. Trust you to get things in a twist!" Temple broke in scathingly. "This gentleman isn't a *bus* inspector any more than I am."

Mr Macready flashed him a look of gratitude. "I'm glad *somebody* has a gleam of common sense," he observed.

"No – he's the gas man," Temple announced triumphantly. "He's come to inspect the meters in the basement."

A cry of horrified protest forced its way through Mr Macready's lips. He reeled with shock and leant against the wall for support. When he had recovered the power of speech he said, "This is preposterous! Have you boys taken leave of your senses? I insist upon seeing the headmaster at once!"

So saying, he turned and marched up the stairs with Temple, Venables and Atkinson trailing behind him. The boys, too, seemed almost as bemused as their guest. If this stranger wasn't the man they assumed him to be, then who on earth was he?

When he reached the top of the stairs and turned into the hall, Mr Macready, though still shaken, began to feel a little easier in his mind. For one thing, he could now see clearly: perhaps, with daylight, sanity would return, and he would find some responsible adult to escort him to the headmaster and explain the nightmare of crossed purposes with which he had been confronted in the basement.

He glanced across the hall and saw, to his relief, a responsible adult approaching at a brisk pace from the far end of the corridor.

"Is this the headmaster?" he inquired.

"No, that's Mr Wilkins, our form master," Temple informed him.

"H'm. It's about time one of the masters turned up," Mr Macready observed. Now, perhaps, he could look forward to receiving a lucid explanation of the incredible way in which he had been treated.

Chapter 16

Thanks to Jennings

There was a forced smile of welcome on Mr Wilkins' face as he advanced with hand outstretched to greet his visitor.

"Ah, good afternoon, Inspector; good afternoon," he said with a heartiness that he was far from feeling. "My name is Wilkins. You – ah – you wish to see me, I believe."

"I certainly do. And before proceeding any further I should like to receive an explanation of . . ."

"Yes, yes, yes, of course," Mr Wilkins broke in hurriedly, as Temple and Atkinson edged a little closer to hear what was going on. He must get rid of these boys at once, he decided. It would never do for the details of his altercation with the police to be broadcast throughout every class in the school. Impatiently, he said, "Run away, you boys, run away. I wish to speak to the inspector privately."

When the scuffle of juvenile footwear had died away in the distance, Mr Wilkins turned again to brave Mr Macready's glance of disapproval.

"I really must apologise for the little misunderstanding," the master began. "But after all it's the sort of thing that might happen to anyone, isn't it? I assure you I had no idea I was breaking the law."

Had everyone taken leave of their senses, Mr Macready wondered! It had been bad enough in the basement with those boys prattling gibberish at the tops of their voices. But this was even more of a shock. He had not expected to find members of the staff behaving in the same half-witted fashion. In a faint voice he queried, "What law, may I inquire?"

"The 'No-waiting' rule, of course. The one that says you can stop on the left-hand side because it's a dotted yellow, but the offside is restricted from Mondays to Saturdays. It's rather awkward, really, stopping on the near side, because you can't turn left at the top by the Town Hall, so you have to go round the block all over again to get into Broad Street."

"What . . . What?" Mr Macready was out of his depth, floundering in a torrent of meaningless words.

"Well, what happened was that I didn't notice the notice, if you follow me." Mr Wilkins gave a little, nervous laugh. "Silly of me, but there it is."

"I don't follow. What notice didn't you notice?"

"The one about the yellow line. It was only a single, of course, not a double. And it wasn't as though it was anywhere near half an hour after sunset. I can show you the lighting-up time in my diary."

Mr Macready raised a restraining hand. He had no wish to see any more diaries. In a daze of bewilderment he listened as Mr Wilkins went on.

"Mind you, I only left it for a few minutes, you know; and when I came back there was one of your chaps waiting for me."

M. D. Macready, Esq, MA (Lond.), had reached the end of his tether. Mindless of his reputation for tact and patience he cried, "This is fantastic! It doesn't make sense! Who are these chaps that everybody seems to think I have at my beck and call? Isn't there anyone in this establishment who possesses a glimmering of intelligence?"

As though in answer to his plea, two grown-up figures

hove into sight round the bend of the corridor. One of them the inspector recognised as the master whom he had met in the staff-room. The other, an older man, hurried forward with the radiant smile and proffered handshake that had proved so misleading when Mr Wilkins had adopted the same tactics a few minutes before.

"How do you do, Mr Macready. I'm the headmaster," Mr Pemberton-Oakes said pleasantly.

The visitor looked at him with deep suspicion. The newcomer seemed harmless enough, but then, so had all the others until they had started to talk. Guardedly, he asked, "You're quite sure of that, I suppose? I mean, you're not going to embark upon a muddle-headed rigmarole about meeting some of my chaps, I trust?"

The smile faded from the headmaster's face. "I beg your pardon?" he said.

"I'm not going to grant any pardons until I know what is going on," returned Mr Macready heatedly. "This really is the most peculiar school I've ever been to. I don't know whether I'm on my head or my heels! First I'm taken down to the cellars to admire the gas-meters; then I'm set upon by some uncouth youth in size five shoes who wants me to read his diary because it's something to do with bus tickets!"

A shocked silence followed this outburst. Then Mr Pemberton-Oakes turned to his assistant and said, "This is most extraordinary. Can you throw any light on what's been happening, Wilkins?"

"It's no good talking to *him*! He's worse than all the boys put together," Mr Macready interposed with some feeling. "He thinks he can't stop on the double-dotted line half an hour before sunset, in case he's offside, or some such nonsense."

The headmaster listened in incredulous dismay. "Wilkins! What have you been saying?"

"Nothing Headmaster, nothing at all," Mr Wilkins defended himself. "I was just telling the police inspector why I parked my car on the wrong side of the road."

"Police!" Mr Pemberton-Oakes clasped his hand to his head and uttered a moan of embarrassment while Mr Macready's eyes grew round with surprise behind his rimless spectacles.

Gently, Mr Carter said, "But, Wilkins, Mr Macready isn't a *police* inspector. He's from the Department of Education and Science. He's come to inspect the work of the school."

"Eh! What? Well, I – I – I!" The hall swam before Mr Wilkins' eyes, and his hand shot to his mouth in sudden realisation. Aghast, he stammered, "Goodness gracious! I – I – I'm terribly sorry. You must have thought I was – well, heaven knows *what* you must have thought. You see, I was told I was wanted by a police officer."

"Who told you that?" Mr Carter inquired.

Once more Mr Wilkins was overcome by a strong emotion. "It was that boy Jennings, that's who it was!" he cried in accents of outraged indignation. "Just wait till I see Master Jennings again! Just wait . . ."

"Quite, quite," the headmaster interposed hurriedly. The situation was delicate enough as it was. A discourse by Mr Wilkins on the shortcomings of a member of the third form would be singularly out of place at the moment.

"Well, now, Mr Macready, if you will come along to my study I'm sure we can straighten out the – ah – little misunderstanding which attended your reception," Mr Pemberton-Oakes said as he led his guest away from the scene of his ordeal.

As a headmaster of long standing, Mr Pemberton-Oakes was well versed in the difficult art of pouring oil on troubled waters. On this occasion his efforts were quickly successful, thanks, chiefly, to the ready co-operation of his visitor.

For Mr Macready was not a man to take offence without cause. As soon as the circumstances had been explained (with the help of statements from Messrs Venables, Temple and Atkinson), he was only too willing to take a light-hearted view of the matter. It would be, he felt, an amusing story with which to regale his colleagues at the D.E.S.

Mr Wilkins, on the other hand, was unable to see any gleam of humour in the situation. Thanks to the stupidity of those silly little boys he had found himself in a very awkward position . . . Very awkward indeed!

He was still wrapped in a pall of gloom when the bell rang for afternoon school and he made his way along to Form Three classroom. At the door he met Mr Carter just returning from the headmaster's study.

"Ah, there you are, Wilkins. Just going into class?" Mr Carter inquired.

His colleague nodded without enthusiasm. "I've got that wretched Form Three for history, this lesson."

"In that case, make sure they're on their toes. The inspector's just been telling the Head that he intends to visit your class during the lesson. History is his subject, you know – his special subject."

Mr Wilkins winced. "This is dreadful, Carter! I can't face that man again, after what happened in the hall this afternoon. Whatever must he be thinking of me? It was too embarrassing for words!"

"Nonsense. In any case, he's got over it. When I saw him

in the Head's study just now, he seemed to think the whole thing was highly amusing."

"Amusing! It's all very well for *him* to make light of it, but how do you think *I* felt? Thanks to that boy Jennings, I've never been so . . ."

"Never mind, Wilkins," Mr Carter broke in. "You'll have a chance to make up for it by showing him what a brilliant history class you've got."

"*Doh!*" Mr Wilkins clutched his head in both hands. "I know what'll happen, Carter. They'll be at their worst – their very worst. He'll go away thinking they're even more dunderheaded than he knows they are already."

Drooping with dejection, Mr Wilkins made his way into the classroom and started writing on the blackboard a genealogical table showing the descent of the Angevin Kings. If he could keep the class busily engaged in written work, there was a chance that the inspector would not ply them with oral questions.

"Copy this down in your best writing," he ordered.

Jennings raised his hand. "Please, sir, it's Friday, sir, and you said you'd . . ."

"Be quiet!" snapped Mr Wilkins. Under normal circumstances he would have remembered the punishment he had set the previous week, but the events of the afternoon had banished the matter from his mind.

"But, sir . . ."

"You heard what I said! Copy this down! I've no intention of wasting half the period listening to your troubles, Jennings. I've got enough of my own."

The lesson had not been in progress for very long when the door opened and Mr Pemberton-Oakes ushered his visitor into the room. His arrival caused a flutter of speculation in certain quarters. Venables, Temple and

Atkinson had already learned from Mr Carter that their hasty conclusions had been somewhat wide of the mark, but Jennings and Darbishire were still unaware of the visitor's real identity.

Darbishire stared at the inspector in awe and wonder . . . Was there, after all, to be a dramatic classroom arrest? It seemed improbable; such things did not happen outside the pages of juvenile fiction . . . Still, there was always a chance!

He felt both relieved and disappointed when the headmaster introduced Mr Macready to the class and revealed the purpose of his visit. Perhaps it was all for the best, Darbishire decided, as Mr Pemberton-Oakes withdrew from the room . . . It was not so exciting, of course: but then, you couldn't have *everything*!

For some minutes after the headmaster had left, Mr Macready strolled round the room peering over the shoulders of the seekers after knowledge, and listening to the clicking and scratching of their pens.

Then, after a brief word with the master in charge, he turned to the class and said, "I see you're studying the latter part of the thirteenth century. A most interesting period, and I'm sure you boys can tell me something about it, eh?"

He paused expectantly, but there was no rush of volunteers eager to embark upon an historical summary of the Plantagenet period.

"Come now," he urged. "Who can suggest, for instance, what it must have been like to have lived in those times?"

Again there was silence. Mr Wilkins groaned inwardly and stared out of the window.

"Nobody? Think now!" The inspector's glance swept round the room and settled on Darbishire, who had been trying to compress himself into the smallest possible space in the hope of being overlooked.

"You, in the back row. Would you like to try and answer my question?"

If he had been asked in the course of a normal lesson, Darbishire might have given a satisfactory answer. But now, with the stranger's eyes fixed upon him, he was seized with a sudden numbness of the brain. He tried to think, but the thoughts would not come. Apart from the fact that there had been no jet aircraft or television sets in those days, he could think of no outstanding examples of the way in which life in the thirteenth century differed from that of modern times.

"I don't really know very much about it, sir," he confessed in a whisper.

Over by the window Mr Wilkins closed his eyes and drew in his breath sharply. Trust Form Three to let him down at the critical moment!

Mr Macready tried again. "Somebody else, then . . . What, *no* volunteers? I'm sure Mr Wilkins has told you quite a lot about England under the Angevins – or Plantagenets, as they are sometimes called."

Form Three shuffled, coughed and relapsed into silence. Calling upon all his reserves of tact and patience, Mr Macready made one last attempt to jog their memories. "Well, one of the most important of the Angevin kings came to the throne in 1272 and . . ."

There was a sudden commotion from the back of the room as a boy leapt to his feet with arm upraised, punching the air above his head in a frantic effort to attract attention.

"What is it?" the inspector inquired.

"Please sir, you mean Edward I, sir? I can tell you absolutely *everything* about him, honestly, sir."

It was the mention of the date 1272 that had released the pent-up stream of knowledge in Jennings' mind. Before that he had listened with uncomprehending ears to such terms as "Angevins" and "Plantagenets" and the "latter part of the thirteenth century". These were meaningless words to Jennings, for the very good reason that none of them happened to occur in the first six pages of Chapter Nine in his history book.

But 1272! That was something he *did* remember. Every day for the past week he had focused his eyes upon the heading: *Edward I, 1272–1307.* He became aware that the inspector was looking at him with interest.

"What is your name?" Mr Macready asked.

"Jennings, sir."

"I see. Well, Jennings, I'm sure we shall be only too pleased to hear what you have to say about the reign of Edward the First."

His moment had come. Jennings stood to attention, cleared his throat and then declaimed in a loud and confident voice.

" 'The reign of Edward the First saw Parliament used for the first time in history as an instrument of government. It was during this reign that great reforms were made in legal matters, for Edward's aim was to make the government of the country strong, and to bring the whole of the British Isles under one rule. In 1275 was passed the first Statute of Westminster . . .' "

The words poured out without hesitation, while Form Three sat back and silently applauded the silver-tongued orator in their midst.

Mr Macready beamed encouragement from the master's desk. Not only was he impressed by the historical accuracy of the recital, but he was also amazed at its fluency. It was remarkable, he thought, that one so young should have such a ready turn of phrase, and such a mature command of language!

Over by the window, Mr Wilkins relaxed with a sigh of relief. It was going to be all right after all!

The hushed room listened with attention as Jennings warmed to his task. In respectful silence they heard him deliver a masterly summary of the first Edwardian era; and all eyes were focused on the speaker as he reached the climax of his lecture.

" '. . . and on the 3rd July, 1307, he set out from Carlisle, but he died within sight of Scotland four days later. With his dying breath he charged his son, Edward, not to bury his bones until the Scots were utterly subdued.

" 'It may be fairly said,' " Jennings concluded in ringing tones, " 'that with the reign of Edward the First begins modern England – the England we know today.' "

There was a short pause to allow the audience to express its appreciation in a buzzing undertone. Then Mr Macready said, "Thank you, Jennings. That was certainly a most admirable answer to my question. I couldn't have done it better myself."

"It was nothing, really, sir," Jennings replied modestly. "Just a few facts I – sort of – happened to remember from what Mr Wilkins told me to do."

"Splendid!" As a rule Mr Macready never expressed his opinion in the presence of staff or pupils, but on this occasion he was so impressed by what he had heard that he turned to the master, now wearing a serene smile in place of his harassed look.

"That was extremely well done, Mr Wilkins. I congratulate you on the thoroughness of your teaching, and the spirit of keenness which you have so obviously instilled. I must confess that when I first came in I found the class a little – er – slow to respond; but once they had got over their shyness – well, you heard the result for yourself."

"Thank you. We do our best, you know," Mr Wilkins said simply.

A glance at the classroom clock warned Mr Macready that it was time for him to go. Other classes were awaiting his attention. At the door he turned and said, "Well done, Jennings! You're a credit to the class."

As the door closed behind the inspector, the buzz of appreciation broke out once more. Mr Wilkins allowed it to run its course. Then he remarked pleasantly, "H'm. Well, that was very gratifying indeed."

"Yes, sir. And it was all thanks to Jennings, wasn't it, sir?" beamed Darbishire.

"Good old Jen! I reckon he deserves a reward," said Atkinson.

"Yes, why not? You could – er – you could . . ." Venables searched his mind for some tribute fitting to the occasion. "I know, sir! You could let him off that punishment you set him last week."

The suggestion was received with wild acclaim. "Oh, yes, sir . . . Really lobsterous idea, sir . . . Why not, sir?"

After all, why not? "Well, yes, I think, in the circumstances, that might be a suitable gesture," Mr Wilkins agreed with a smile.

Jennings was shocked by this outrageous suggestion.

"Oh *no*, sir! That's not fair, sir," he protested indignantly. "You can't let me off my punishment *now*, sir. It's too late. You've just heard me say it – all six pages without a prompt!"

Form Three nodded in approval. On second thoughts they agreed that a reprieve, after the sentence had been

,carried out, would be an extravagant waste of a perfectly good punishment.

"Of course, I know what you *could* do instead, sir," Jennings said slowly as an alternative came into his mind. "You could owe me a punishment, sir."

"*Owe* you one?" Mr Wilkins echoed blankly.

"Yes, sir. You could call it punishment in advance, sir," Jennings explained. "So next time I do anything wrong you could agree not to say anything about it, and then we shall be all square again, sir."

"Well, – I – I . . . Of all the . . . I never heard such a fantastic suggestion in my life!"

Mr Wilkins' mild expostulations were interrupted by the bell for the end of the period. He picked up his books and made his way slowly towards the staff common room, shaking his head in puzzled wonder . . . Punishment in advance, indeed! . . . *Tut*! What extraordinary ideas these boys got into their heads. The more he saw of Jennings the less he understood the way in which his mind appeared to work.

The door of the common room opened as he approached, and Mr Carter strolled out on his way to take Form Three for the next period.

"Well, Wilkins, have a good history lesson?" he asked in a jocular tone.

The answer was unexpected. "Yes, rather. Everything went splendidly – thanks to Jennings."

Mr Carter raised one eyebrow. "You surprise me!" he said.

In point of fact, Mr Wilkins had rather surprised himself with the phrase which had sprung to his lips; and he stood thinking about it long after his colleague had disappeared round the bend of the corridor.

For it was thanks to Jennings that the orderly routine of the school – to say nothing of his own peace of mind – so often broke down in chaos and confusion. The trouble he had been caused over the disappearing guinea-pig; the turmoil he had had to put up with on the organised outing; the embarrassment he had endured at his meeting with the so-called police officer – all these were thanks to Jennings.

And yet, Mr Wilkins reminded himself as he opened the staff-room door – and yet, it was also thanks to Jennings that the fateful lesson had been such an outstanding success, and that Her Majesty's Inspector had gone away deeply impressed with Form Three's progress in history.

If Jennings could claim credit for *that*, Mr Wilkins reflected as he closed the door behind him, then surely there must be *something* to be said for the silly little boy, after all!

Anthony Buckeridge
Jennings Goes to School

'Why do these frantic hoo-hahs always have to pick on us to happen to?' said Darbishire.

Linbury Court School could never have imagined what was in store when it welcomed two of its new boys. For Jennings and Darbishire soon prove they have a talent for trouble when their brilliant schemes go disastrously awry!

First there's their clever plan to escape from school, and then the little incident with the giant killer spider . . .

The first book in the classic Jennings series – some of the funniest school stories ever written.

'Jennings is great!' *The Times*